Nothing is ever really safe, Leticia thought as she swept her flashlight back and forth like a lighthouse beam. She watched as Mrs. Donnelley and Ty crossed the street to ring another doorbell. Mrs. Donnelley was not really safe. She was too phony, and her home was hot and pink and bright and strange and slightly unwelcoming, no matter how many times Leticia had stayed over.

And Martha was not safe, either. Martha would do anything to get her way.

Suddenly, Serena squeezed her elbow. "Teesh, I'm scared!" she said. "It sounds weird. Listen."

Ty and Mrs. Donnelley and Topher and some of the neighbors were calling Gray's name. Gray's name was a single sound that did not stop.

Graaaaaaaaaaaaaaaaaaaaaaaaaaaaaaaaaaaaaaaaaaaaaaaay!

A lost, lonely sound, thought Leticia.

She hoped Gray was safe, wherever she was.

↩

OTHER SPEAK BOOKS

Overnight

Adele Griffin

speak

An Imprint of Penguin Group (USA) Inc.

SPEAK

Published by Penguin Group

Penguin Group (USA) Inc.,

345 Hudson Street, New York, New York 10014, U.S.A.

Penguin Books Ltd, 80 Strand, London WC2R ORL, England

Penguin Books Australia Ltd, 250 Camberwell Road,

Camberwell, Victoria 3124, Australia

Penguin Books Canada Ltd, 10 Alcorn Avenue, Toronto, Ontario, Canada M4V 3B2

Penguin Books (N.Z.) Ltd, 182-190 Wairau Road, Auckland 10, New Zealand

First published in the United States of America by G. P. Putnam's Sons,
a division of Penguin Putnam Books for Young Readers, 2003
Published by Speak, an imprint of Penguin Group (USA) Inc., 2004

1 3 5 7 9 10 8 6 4 2

THE LIBRARY OF CONGRESS HAS CATALOGED THE G. P. PUTNAM'S EDITION AS FOLLOWS:

Griffin, Adele.

Overnight / Adele Griffin.

p.   cm.

Summary: Gray hopes that going to a slumber party with the "Lucky Seven" at her
private school will take her mind off her mother's cancer, but when she is taken from
the party by a deranged woman, both she and the other girls
discover things about themselves and each other.

ISBN: 0-399-23782-8 (hc)

[1. Cliques (Sociology)—Fiction. 2. Interpersonal relations—Fiction.
3. Kidnapping—Fiction. 4. Sleepovers—Fiction.]

I. Title.

PZ7.G881325 Ov 2003

[Fic]—dc21   2002069778

Speak ISBN 0-14-240143-9

Printed in the United States of America

For Charlotte

Overnight

Gray

Gray forgot her sleeping bag for Caitlin Donnelley's birthday party. She did not see that it was missing until her mother pulled up to the front doors of Fielding Academy. When she reached for her overnight things piled in the backseat, it was not there.

"My sleeping bag!" she exclaimed. "I left it at home!"

"Oh, for goodness' sakes, Gray." Her mother sighed. "How could you be so forgetful?"

"Please, Mom, go back!"

"If I go back, you'll both be late for school."

"Mom, it's important!"

In the backseat, Gray's younger brother, Robby, began to whimper. He was seven, four years younger than Gray, and he copied whatever she did.

Mrs. Rosenfeld rested her forehead on the steering wheel, practicing her yoga breathing to keep calm. When she lifted her head, she said, "Gray, get out of the car this instant so that I can drop off Robby at school. Then I will go home and collect your sleeping bag and I will bring it to Fielding later this morning."

"You know which one! The pink one with the fairies on it!" Gray insisted as her mother drove away. Her breath, damp and fast, made icy puffs in the February cold. "Not any of the other ones! The pink one!" Her voice was lost to the car, but she continued shouting through her fingertips as it disappeared. The last thing she saw was Robby mouthing teary good-byes from the rearview window.

Later that morning, one of the school secretaries delivered Gray's sleeping bag to the sixth-grade classroom. It was not her fairy-folk bag. It was the navy blue bag that her father took on fishing trips.

When Caitlin Donnelley and Kristy Sonenshine saw it, they exchanged google eyes and stuck out their tongues at each other. Gray saw them do this and it made her feel dizzy, as if she might throw up. Worse, she would have to sleep without her fairy folk. Gray liked to believe that at night, while she fit snug inside the bag, the fairies came alive.

Alive like real people but better joining together hand in hand in an enchanted circle protecting me from all bad things.

Gray knew it was a babyish thought. She even knew it was a babyish bag. Plain pastels or wildflower prints were the only acceptable sleeping bag styles this year. Part of her, though, especially her nighttime, lights-off part, needed the fairies.

The navy bag looked twice the size of the other girls' bags. It smelled like the woods and was dark as a midnight ocean.

Who would protect her now?

Mrs. Donnelley was waiting to catch the girls as they spilled out of Fielding Academy's front doors at the school day's end.

"Hello there, Miss Gray! How's your mom? I meant to call her yesterday."

"Oh. She's fine."

Mrs. Donnelley nodded hard, as if her head were being jerked by puppet strings. Yes yes yes—casting a spell that would make the cancer leave. In that way, Gray's mother and Mrs. Donnelley were alike. They both put Safety first. Safety first and no mistakes, which was why Gray's mother and Caitlin's mother were friends. Gray had slept over at Caitlin Donnelley's house lots of times, and she had watched Mrs. Donnelley's struggle to make each detail of her home perfect, indoors and out. Each dead leaf picked quickly off the yard and every slice of toast crisped tan.

The way my mom used to be but not anymore.

As girls trundled outside, lugging their sleeping bags, Mrs. Donnelley gave instructions. "I can take four, so that means three of you girls must go with Topher in his car. I don't have enough seat belts to buckle up everybody!"

She pointed across the parking lot to where Topher was leaning against the side of his battered Volkswagen. Topher was Caitlin's half brother. He was in college and home for mid-winter break. He had a goatee. When he laughed, he crossed his arms and tipped back his head like a genie. Gray had known Topher since she was five years old, and she still did not like to talk much when he was around.

Quickly, Gray jumped into the minivan so that she could sit right behind Mrs. Donnelley. The three girls who clambered in after her were Leticia Watkins, Serena Hodgson, and Zoë Atacropolis. Zoë sat up front so that she could talk Mrs. Donnelley's ear off. Topher would be taking Caitlin and Kristy and Martha Van Riet. Already they were crossing the parking lot, Kristy springing next to Caitlin like a puppy and Martha snaking up behind them.

Seven girls in all. Of the fifty-one sixth-graders enrolled at Fielding Academy for Girls, they were the "Lucky Seven." That's what they called themselves. Other girls called them the "cool group." Or the "in crowd." Or the "snobby girls." Or "Martha's group." Or "*those* girls."

Gray looked out the window to where some of the uninvited girls were standing, plumped in wool coats, waiting for buses and carpools. The uninvited girls, eyes lowered, watched as Mrs. Donnelley's minivan and Topher's Volkswagen circled the parking lot, and their faces pretended indifference. After all, it was Friday! The weekend! Who cared about Caitlin Donnelley? Oh, they weren't missing anything much!

Gray knew what they were thinking behind their faces. This

past fall, when she had been nearly expelled from the Lucky Seven and Martha had not invited her to her roller-skating party, Gray had thought those same kinds of thoughts.

Annie Dearborne, slumped on the bus bench, raised her hand to wave good-bye. Annie was Gray's writing comprehension partner. When Gray was having problems with the Lucky Seven, Annie Dearborne almost had become Gray's new best friend. Almost.

Before anyone else saw, Gray flicked her fingers good-bye at Annie. Then she turned away. She pushed her seat forward so that she could smell the perfume at the back of Mrs. Donnelley's neck. She used the tips of her shoes to pedal her wrong sleeping bag deeper under the driver's-side seat and she clicked on her seat belt very loud so that Mrs. Donnelley would hear and appreciate Gray's carefulness.

"It's all a mistake. How could this be?" Gray's mother had asked this question in the hospital last spring, Robby tucked on one side of her and Gray curled up on the other, though the bed was too narrow and one of Gray's legs was getting cold, pressed-jammed hard into the bed's metal side rails.

Gray had thought her mother meant how could this be that she was lying in this bed, in this hospital. A mistake, because she wasn't sick after all!

Later, Gray understood what her mother really meant. That no matter how Safe a person tried to be, cancer was a mistake forced on a few unlucky people.

"We're having pizza!" exclaimed Mrs. Donnelley.

"And cake and ice cream?" asked Leticia.

"And are there goody bags?" asked Serena.

"And do we get to watch movies?" asked Zoë.

"Of course!" Mrs. Donnelley's voice trilled, filling the car with promises.

"Yes!"

"Yes!"

"Yes!"

Gray adored Caitlin's room. The furniture was quaint, like *Little House on the Prairie* if Ma and Pa Ingalls had been rich. Mrs. Donnelley had decorated it herself and kept the room pin-straight, the curtains and canopy bed freshly fluffed and vacuum marks on the carpet. There was a Victorian dollhouse in one corner and a pigeonhole desk in another corner. Neither of these pieces was used, since both were antiques. Besides, Caitlin had hated her dolls since she was nine—had hated everything about her room, in fact, since she was ten—and she did all her homework on the computer at her built-in study unit.

What Gray loved most about Caitlin's room were Caitlin's fairy paintings. There were four paintings altogether, one for every wall and season. These were not silly cartoon pictures, either, but framed portraits of ravishing enchantresses with dewy eyes, veined wings, and the tingling of the outdoors in their cheeks.

The winter fairy, dressed in cobwebby white, lounged like a fashion model along the branch of an icicle-spiked tree.

Two spring fairies chased each other in a daisy field under an azure sky.

The summer fairy kneeled on a lily pad, absorbed in her watery reflection.

The autumn fairies were gathered around the stump of a tree, some leaning against cushions, their faces serious, as if they were at a Seder.

Autumn was Gray's least favorite picture and the one she stared at most. But the autumn fairies did not fit with the other paintings. For one thing, the painting was overcrowded, and not just with fairies, but spindly-legged frogs and hunchbacked gnomes and pop-eyed hobgoblins and even one leering, rickety cricket.

For years, ever since Gray had first started staying overnight at Caitlin's house, she had put herself to sleep wondering about those ugly autumn wood creatures. Why had the fairies invited them to their Seder? Why? Why? She would stare and stare until her eyes lidded over.

"Come on, Gray! Drop your bags! We're going down to play Enchanted Castle." Caitlin nudged Gray from her trance. "Stop looking at that picture. Did I tell you I get to redo my room any way I want for a birthday present? Dad and Mom said okay, even for humongous posters and a futon, if I want."

"That's cool," said Martha. " 'Cause your room sucks."

"Duh! I know!" Caitlin laughed shrilly. "Whatever, though! It's changing in, like, a week!"

The other girls tossed down their bags and changed quickly from their uniforms into jeans and sweaters. Giggling and pushing, they herded out the door. Then down the hall, down the stairs, and down the stairs again to the family room in the basement.

Gray listened to them go. Alone in Caitlin's room, she changed clothes and sighed. The other girls' sleeping bags were so pretty, so *right*. Pale rainbow colors or tiny sprigs of flowers. Gray dropped her stupid, ugly sleeping bag and kicked it hard as a soccer ball under Caitlin's bed, hiding it from sight. She despised the idea of sliding into it tonight, trapped inside a giant's stinky sock while everyone else was tucked into butterfly cocoons.

Hot, easy tears welled up in her eyes. It wasn't fair. It wasn't fair that this new version of her mother made so many mistakes. Mistakes on account of her sickness, mistakes that might seem silly or thoughtless but also were careless enough to hurt.

The others already had set up the Enchanted Castle board by the time Gray joined them in the family room. Gray frowned as she slid into her chair. Enchanted Castle was dull. The object of the game was either to capture the Evil Queen or to find her three treasures—her crystal ball, her golden nightingale, and her jeweled crown, all of which were hidden somewhere in her kingdom. But if the Evil Queen managed to lock up three princesses in the dungeon, then she won.

The Evil Queen had the best time of anyone. This afternoon, the Queen was Caitlin, obviously. Gray was surprised that Caitlin wanted to play Enchanted Castle at all, especially with Martha rolling her eyes and saying, "Ugh, Caitlin, it's so spanky, so loserish, this game."

Caitlin insisted, though. Maybe just to be stubborn, or maybe since it was her birthday. Or maybe because she really liked Enchanted Castle and she knew that today was one of the few times she could get away with making everyone participate.

On her third turn, Gray began to feel sleepy, the same stupor that sometimes overcame her during afternoon classes. She could hardly keep her eyes open.

"I don't really want to play Enchanted Castle anymore," she said. "If that's all right with you, Caitlin?" She figured it would be. If she quit, Caitlin had a better chance of winning.

Caitlin shrugged. "Okay."

But Martha sang, "Rainy Gray, go away, come again some other day—*not!*"

Gray took her princess off the board and stood. She ignored Martha. To say something back meant trouble. Martha always shot the dart that started a fight. And Martha never let go. Last year, Martha had been so nasty to Beth Terrene that by March, Beth had transferred from Fielding Academy to Saint

Carmela's. She said it was because her grades were bad. Which was probably true. How could Beth have concentrated on school with Martha Van Riet making every second of her life more miserable than the last?

Most of the time, the girls brushed aside Martha's jabs and stabs, otherwise she'd be at them all day long.

On the couch, Caitlin's younger brother, Ty, was watching race-car driving, clenching his hands and whispering, "Go go go! Turbocharge it! Pedal to the metal!"

Gray flopped onto the couch and Ty scooted over obligingly. "It's the Daytona Five Hundred," he told her. He seemed so spellbound that Gray did not have the heart to ask him to switch the channel to see what else was on.

Around and around went the cars, the same thing again and again. Gray wondered what else there was to do. Everything seemed dumb and boring, she was hungry and she itched to wander. Maybe she would sneak up to Caitlin's room and look through her bookshelf.

"Would you like something to drink?" she asked Ty. "I'm going to the kitchen."

Ty looked up, startled from his sports trance. "Uh. Grape juice," he said. "No. Cranapple."

"Be right back." She stood, undecided whether to ask if anyone else wanted a drink. "Does anyone want, like, a snack or something from the kitchen?" But the other girls seemed too absorbed in Enchanted Castle to answer. Or they were being rude on purpose. Ignoring Gray was a game the group sometimes ganged up to play against her. "Save my seat," she said, to nobody.

Gray walked upstairs to the empty kitchen. The polished glass sliding doors that looked out over the Donnelleys' backyard and swimming pool were now solidly dark, creating a mirror effect, doubling the image of the kitchen's gleaming chrome. She flipped on a light and flipped it off again.

Upstairs, Gray heard Mrs. Donnelley and Topher talking and laughing. That was nice. Gray knew that Mrs. Donnelley was not Topher's real mom. Topher's real mom was some lady who had been married to Mr. Donnelley a long time ago, who lived somewhere else now and was not part of this Donnelley family.

Abruptly, Gray wondered what kind of lady her dad would choose if her mother died and he got remarried. What were the chances that she and Robby would have a stepmother as nice as Mrs. Donnelley? Even as Gray tried to picture different mothers—all her friends' mothers came to mind—she felt awful, like a traitor, a cheat, jinxing her own mother's chances to get all the way better.

Gray pushed aside the vision of the other mothers.

Would she be in trouble if she helped herself and Ty to some juice? Would Mrs. Donnelley mind? She opened a cupboard and was confronted with rows and rows of sparkly clean glasses. Mrs. Donnelley's house had so many rules! There was probably a special glass for each type of drink.

She closed the cupboard and noticed the phone on the wall next to the refrigerator. Maybe she would call home and tell her mother to come by with her fairy-folk bag. Although her dad would be angry if he found out. Gray and Robby weren't supposed to bother their mother with extra errands and requests and lists of "I need."

Well, so what? So what if he was angry? It was her mother's mistake, after all. Gray picked up the phone and punched in her home number.

Four rings and then the answering machine. She left a message.

"Mom, it's me at Caitlin's. Will you please bring me my right sleeping bag? You brought the wrong one to school. I need *my* one, my pink one. You know which, with fairies on it." She was trying not to whine and her voice sounded clogged at the base. She hung up the phone. From behind, she felt the prickling tug of being watched, although when she glanced around, nobody was in sight. The kitchen was quiet, gleaming, humming. Like a shut-down space station, Gray thought.

She opened the refrigerator. All this food! Cartons and bottles and tubs and containers of it, neatly wrapped and normal looking. No dark spinach and organic glop like what her mother ate now, for her health. The only problem was that

none of the Donnelleys' food looked easy to get to. Even the
bottle of Cranapple juice Ty wanted was unopened, sealed
around its lip with a thin, clear, childproof band.

A crisper filled with fruit seemed most promising. Gray slid
open the drawer and pinched a bunch of fat purple grapes.
They tasted okay, but coming from such a perfect refrigerator,
she felt a brief flicker of disappointment that they should have
been fruitier, cleaner, better.

She closed the refrigerator door.

A tattered apparition stood outside, behind the sliding doors.
A woman. Gray's heart jumped and her throat closed and she
started to choke on her grape. As she coughed, the woman's
eyes rounded and her mouth dropped into an *O* that looked too
big for her shocked face.

Gray stopped coughing and the woman's mouth shut. She
had sad eyes and long, ropy brown hair tied back in a handkerchief. Underneath her layers of clothing—a baggy dress and
a rust-orange-colored coat with a feathery trim—she was
knife-thin. Gray could see the bones of her neck and wrists,
the shadows scooped into her cheeks and temples.

Now the woman rapped her knuckles on the glass and mo-
tioned for Gray to let her inside. Gray stared. She did not recognize the woman as a friend of Mrs. Donnelley's. She did not
recognize the woman as a mother from school, either—although she was about the same age as a mother. Perhaps she
was one of the Donnelleys' next-door neighbors? Like Mrs.

Nuñez, who lived across the street from the Rosenfelds? Mrs. Nuñez wore safety-pinned bath towels as skirts and she never turned off her radio and she strung Christmas lights in her holly bushes all year long. Gray's parents called Mrs. Nuñez "a real piece of work" and always wished she would move away.

Maybe this woman also was "a real piece of work"?

Gray paused another moment, then crossed the kitchen, unlocked and slid open the door. The woman did not move. "Hello, you!" she exclaimed in a soft, curious voice. "Am I late? I saw the balloons."

"Oh, those are for Caitlin. It's her birthday party."

"I've been driving around and around, looking for the party. When I saw the balloons, I guessed I was at the right place." The woman stared at Gray expectantly.

"Do you want to come inside?" Gray wondered if this was the right thing to ask. She was not stupid. She knew all the rules about not talking to strangers.

The woman seemed harmless, though. She stepped delicately into the kitchen as if it were stuffed with people, not just herself and Gray. She kept her back pressed against the glass wall. Her eyes darted from counter to counter. "Oh, I don't like it here. It's different on the inside. I like more lights, maybe a radio. This isn't my party, after all."

"Are you a neighbor?" Gray asked.

"Yes," said the woman. "Do you live here?"

"No. And I need to go home," Gray blurted out. Tears souped her eyes. "I have to pick up my sleeping bag."

"Of course." The woman agreed as if she knew that already. "I think we'd better go now." She held out her hand for Gray to take. "All set?"

"Oh!" Gray smiled. "Are you here for me? Are you from Helping Hands?"

"Yes, that's right."

No. That couldn't be right. This woman did not look like a Helping Hands person, and Gray had met quite a few of them. Last year, when her mother had been very sick, Helping Hands people had been around a lot of the time. Mostly women, but there had been one man, Brett. They all were nice, especially Ann Lee and Moira, although Moira could get impatient if Gray didn't know the directions to soccer practice or kept her waiting too long in the Fielding parking lot.

This woman could not be a Helping Hands lady. Also, Gray's parents did not use the Helping Hands service anymore, now that her mother was recovering.

Or do we use it but only sometimes because maybe Mom picked up my message and called in for a Helping Hands person for just this once this one important errand?

"We're going to get my sleeping bag and come right back?" Gray asked.

"Yes," said the woman. She snapped her fingers. "We need to hurry. I have a lot of other things to do."

Zoë

Zoë was going to win. She was the best. She knew that. Besides, the other girls did not care as much about winning. Their hearts did not flutter when the Enchanted Castle game board was opened. Their mouths did not dry up when the scorecards were laid out, neat as buttons, all in a row. Their fingers did not sweat with each roll of the dice.

I'll win this game, Zoë thought. Yes, yes! Because I always win this game.

From the start, though, Zoë sensed that Kristy was trying to tip off the table to let Caitlin win. Kristy Kiss-up, that's what Martha called Kristy behind her back because of how she acted toward Caitlin. Sure enough, when Caitlin got up to go to the bathroom, Kristy leaned forward.

"You guys, it's Caitlin's birthday," Kristy whispered, "and she never wins. Let's let her beat us this once."

No, no! thought Zoë. Not fair! Caitlin had too much luck already. Caitlin was a girl who always had the right sneakers, the right hair bands and clips, even the right day—Valentine's Day!—for her birthday. The right mother, too, because Mrs. Donnelley was perfect. Mrs. Donnelley, who wore thigh-length tennis dresses, whose legs were shiny, moisturized, and tan—even in winter—and who picked up Caitlin at school on time every afternoon. And who, glamorous as she was, never was doing anything so important that she couldn't interrupt herself to perform even the silliest, smallest errand for Caitlin.

Caitlin didn't need to win! No fair!

"Gosh, I think letting Caitlin beat us is a sweet idea, Kristy," said Martha in a honeyed voice. She winked at Zoë and pursed her lips into a kiss. Zoë swallowed and clenched her fists and was silent.

"That's cheating," countered Leticia, "and I won't play if the game is *fixed!*"

Serena sighed prettily and shook back her thick ginger hair. "I agree."

"Me, too," said Zoë, relaxing her hands. Ha, ha, you lose, Martha.

"Oh, you're all such morons," said Martha. "Like it matters who wins! Like it means anything!"

"Yeah, have it your own dumb way," said Kristy. "Here comes Caitlin back, so shut up about it."

On Kristy's next turn, Zoë watched as she picked up a card and rubbed her nose. She must have found one of the Queen's treasures. Kristy was easy to read. She had so many tics and twitchy habits.

Yawning, Kristy replaced the card in the Throne Room. Zoë, her own face blank, made a mental note of it.

When Gray quit the game, Zoë's victory was assured. Gray was good at Enchanted Castle. She paid attention and followed the rules.

Zoë watched as Gray mumbled some excuse and retreated to the couch. She looked worn and sunk.

What was wrong with Gray these days? Her mom was supposed to be cured, or at least close to cured. So it couldn't be that.

Zoë would not be the one to bring it up. She had learned her lesson this past fall when she had found Gray crying in the bathroom. Concerned, she had made the mistake of telling the others in the group. As a friend! As a friend was why she told!

"Poor Gray! She was crying in the stall next to mine. What do you think's the matter? Do you think it's about her mom?"

"Gray's such a lick," Martha had answered. "I bet I could make her cry just by staring at her."

Then Martha had stared at Gray all through lunch, unsmiling, unspeaking, until Gray had collapsed in tears. "Why are you doing that, Martha? Stop watching me!"

That was how the game started. Stare-at-Gray-till-she-cried. Ignore-Gray-till-she-cried. It was sort of funny but not really. Then Martha didn't invite Gray to her skating party. Eventually, Gray was pretty much nudged out of the Lucky Seven, but last month she had drifted back in. Probably on account of Caitlin's influence, Zoë figured. Caitlin's and Gray's moms had been friends forever, so Caitlin and Gray used to be best friends when they were little.

Zoë bet next year would be different. These days, Caitlin and Kristy were stuck together like peanut butter and jelly. And Gray sometimes acted like a *lick*, she was too *spanky*, she could be *unc;* all Lucky Seven words that Zoë herself had made up. It was Martha who loved to use the words Zoë had invented for the group. Zoë didn't. Not on Gray, anyway. Gray's feelings got hurt too easy.

After Gray went upstairs, Martha turned to Zoë and said, "I bet she's pigging down the cake."

Zoë laughed, though it made her feel guilty. Gray was small and underweight, but she was always hungry, always eating in the same rabbity, bad-habit way that Zoë bit her nails. But Zoë laughed because there was something magnetic about Martha when she was joking and friendly. Her eyes sparkled like gold firecrackers, a change that warmed her hard, flat face.

"Gray can eat the whole entire cake and she'll never gain a pound," Caitlin said. "My mom always makes stuff low-fat, so that I can watch my figure."

Zoë thought it was cool that Mrs. Donnelley was already thinking about Caitlin's figure. It made Caitlin seem mature.

"I have a really good metabolism, so I can eat whatever I want," Zoë said.

"Ugh, Zoë, you get High Honors every single report card. Isn't that enough? Why does everything have to be a competition with you?" snapped Martha. She began talking in an announcer's voice. "And now, Fielding Academy's prize for Best Metabolism this year goes to—Zoë Atacropolis! Again, folks! Amazing!"

Everyone laughed. Zoë smiled, but only to show she was a good sport.

Sometimes, secretly, Zoë wanted out of the Lucky Seven. Even if it was the best, the most popular group, sometimes the group did not seem fun enough for the effort it took to stay in it. The problem was that if she dropped out, then she would be a quitter. Maybe even a loser. Two things her older brother, Shelton, would never let himself be.

Martha was talking into her microphone fist, still acting like a broadcaster. "This is Miss Atacropolis's sixth straight year of winning Best Meta—"

"Hey, would you shut up, Martha?" Leticia interrupted. "I can't concentrate."

The others stopped laughing.

Martha stopped talking. She looked surprised.

Nobody spoke. Everyone watched as Leticia drew a card and finished her turn.

"Go, Kristy," she said, pushing the dice.

And so the game continued.

Martha

Martha noticed that Gray had been gone for a while.

"Where is Mouse?" she asked. Mouse was Martha's special behind-her-back name for Gray, because she was so small and squeaky.

Caitlin smirked. "Who cares? The fun is here, and the Evil Queen shall win all."

Martha rolled her eyes. Caitlin was getting on her nerves, using too much time on her turn and cackling, "I'll get you, my pretty!" when it was anyone else's. Enchanted Castle sucked for anyone who wasn't the Evil Queen, and it looked as if Zoë was going to win. Zoë, as usual.

"Gray!" Martha shouted so loud that Serena, sitting next to her, had to cover her ears.

"Gray went upstairs to get me some juice," called Ty from the couch. "But that was a long time ago. Like half an hour ago."

"Shut up!" yelled Caitlin. "You're breaking the rule! You butt in and say one single more thing and I'll make Mom send you out of here to watch TV in your room forever!"

Zoë pointed to Martha. "Your turn, Mar."

Martha rolled doubles and moved her princess into the Hall of Mirrors.

"I'll get you, my pretty!" screeched Caitlin for the thousandth time. "And your little dog, too!"

"Caitlin, do you know how goddamn annoying that is?" asked Martha.

The table hushed. Martha smiled. Bad words were plentiful as rocks and just as easy to throw; they hardly took any nerve at all and she didn't know why people found them so startling.

But they did.

All the noise left in the room was the sound of the television, of race cars roaring around the track.

"Girls! Ty!" shouted Mrs. Donnelley. "Pizza!"

"I'm gonna eat all you girls' pizza!" Ty stretched his arms. "Chomp chomp chomp! I could eat sixty gazillion slices right now!"

"That's it, Ty!" Caitlin sprang from her chair, knocking it over, and rushed her brother. She flung herself over the back of the couch to cuff Ty hard from behind with the flat of her hand. "Shut up, shut up, dumb third-grader vomit face!"

"Caitlin, come back," implored Zoë.

Zoë was two turns away from winning, and Martha could tell Caitlin was glad for any interruption.

"I hate you, Ty!" screamed Caitlin at the top of her lungs.

"Ha ha ha ha ha! You're not s'posed to say *hate!* I'm telling!" Ty jounced up from the couch to yank a fistful of his sister's hair so hard that he came away with loose strands like shucked corn. "Painful, ainnit? Painful, ainnit?" he yelled, lunging for more.

As Caitlin started screeching loud as an ambulance siren, Ty changed his mind and jumped off the couch and up the stairs. Martha watched him leap out of reach before Caitlin could bite or scratch him. She gave chase anyway.

"I guess the game is over?" asked Zoë. "I guess I won?"

"Nuh-uh, nobody won, stupid." Martha despised how Zoë sort-of pretended how she didn't care about winning when really she wanted it more than anything.

Mrs. Donnelley and Topher were in the dining room, working on the table's finishing touches. Topher was a hottie, Martha thought. He had not been noticing her nearly as much as she wished. She half closed her eyes and tilted her head and put her hands on her hips, but still he didn't notice.

Mrs. Donnelley had prepared the room with a pink paper tablecloth and pink napkins. There were pink paper plates and cups and pink plastic forks and spoons. Seven pink crepe-paper streamers tied from the chandelier looped a path to a goody bag at each place setting. Pink, pink, pink, because Caitlin was born on Valentine's Day, which would be tomorrow.

Mrs. Donnelley began ticking off names as the girls settled into their seats. "Serena, Zoë, Martha, Leticia, Kristy, and Caitlin, my birthday girl!" She pointed to the empty place setting and asked, "Who is missing?"

"Gray," Martha answered promptly.

"Oh, yes!" Mrs. Donnelley smiled. "Where is Gray?"

"She's in the kitchen, getting me some juice," said Ty. He was standing at the sideboard, scooping Valentine red hots into his mouth and pockets.

"No one's in the kitchen," said Topher as he plowed through the swinging door with a soda bottle in each hand. Diet grape and diet orange.

"I'm not allowed to drink anything carbonated," said Leticia.

"I'm not allowed to drink anything diet," said Martha. This was not true, but she liked to see the anxiety pulse in Mrs. Donnelley's face.

"That's why there's lemonade on the table. *My pretty!*" squealed Caitlin, protected by her mother's presence and staring Martha down.

"I'm allergic to peanuts," said Zoë. She reminded people of this constantly.

"Ty, go find Gray," ordered Mrs. Donnelley. "Hurry, hurry! And don't eat those!"

Ty shook one more handful of red hots into his mouth and galloped out of the dining room. Mrs. Donnelley turned a proud eye on the table.

"Doesn't this look wonderful? As soon as Gray is here, we'll be perfect."

Martha smiled a tiny closed-lips smile, and her heart flipped pleasantly. She had a feeling that something was going wrong. Gray really should have come back by now.

In a few minutes, everyone was shouting for Gray.

Everyone except Martha.

She stayed in her seat as the room emptied.

As soon as she was alone, Martha switched her goody bag for Serena's bag, which was stuffed fat as a pincushion with the most candy. To make sure Serena didn't trade back, Martha opened the bag, selected a heart-shaped chocolate, and dropped it into her mouth. The chocolate smeared on her fingers because the Donnelleys' house was too warm.

The heart tasted plasticky but was liquid on the inside. Martha let the chocolate muddle over her tongue and bleed down her throat, warm and thin and sweet.

Nice, nice enough.

Mr. Donnelley came home.

"I'm home!" he shouted. He kicked the front door shut with

his heel, twisting the corner of the carpet runner as he did so, a rude guest in his own house.

Martha, nauseated from having eaten three more chocolate hearts, had slid out of her chair when she heard his car in the driveway. Now she leaned against the dining room door, half hidden by it, watching.

The family rushed Mr. Donnelley from all sides as if he'd just caught the pass in a football game. Nobody saw Martha.

"Daddy, my friend Gray is missing!" yelled Caitlin.

"Daddy, Topher says we should call the cops!" yelled Ty.

"I've been trying the car! I've been trying your cell phone!" Mrs. Donnelley nearly tripped and fell as she rushed down the stairs. "Go, go on, Caitlin, Ty. Leave me to talk to Daddy alone."

Martha hardly dared a breath. She made her eyes stony and unblinking. On their mother's push, Caitlin and Ty slipped away into the kitchen and then could be heard outside, shouting for Gray again.

Now it was just the three of them.

Mr. Donnelley's arms were weighted with his overcoat and his briefcase, so Mrs. Donnelley could not touch him. Her hands twisted together and she spoke in a jabber.

"One of the girls has wandered off. You know Gray. Into thin air. I was up in the attic, cobwebs all over me, on any chance she might have—"

"Maybe she's asleep somewhere in the house. By the way, we lost the appeal."

"Honey, I'm so sorry."

Mr. Donnelley handed over his overcoat with a grunt. "Do you mind? I'm dead on my feet."

"Yes, you look exhausted." Mrs. Donnelley took the coat and opened the hall closet. "I've searched the house top to bottom, the attic, everywhere. Topher is trying to keep the girls from running down the street. It's chaos. And I can't get hold of the Rosenfelds." She selected a heavy wooden hanger from its bar and hung the coat, smoothing it carefully into place with the others. "Should we call the police? What should we do?"

"Let me shower and change. Then I'll decide."

Martha thought Mr. Donnelley resembled an old profes-sional wrestler. He was big and ruddy and balding, with the same wide clown mouth as Caitlin. Bad luck for Caitlin.

After Mr. Donnelley went upstairs, Mrs. Donnelley spied Martha. A wisp of frown crossed her face, though her tone was pleasant as she asked, "Martha, sweetie, do you have any idea where Miss Gray might have wandered off to?"

Martha pretended to think. "Maybe she walked home? She seemed . . . depressed. She didn't want to play Enchanted Castle with us. Gosh, I hope she didn't try to walk along the high-way!"

She watched this bright new fear touch down in Mrs.

Donnelley's eyes. Martha enjoyed the game of digging to the secret fears inside people.

In fact, today had been a great day for secrets. Today, Martha had caught hold of her best secret yet. And it had been Mrs. Donnelley's fault, sort of. Mrs. Donnelley, who, earlier this afternoon, after directing all the girls out of the minivan and Topher's car and instructing them to put their overnight and sleeping bags in Caitlin's room, had exclaimed, "Oh, gosh! The mail! Darn! Could someone run down and get the mail?" She had pointed to Martha. "Sweetie? Do you mind?"

Martha did not mind. She had run outside again, all the way down to the edge of the lawn, to the mailbox tied with bobbing pink balloons, and collected the mail.

The lady had been standing right at the bottom of the driveway. She had long thick hair like yarn and her face and lips were sparkly and she was wearing a feathery orange coat. She waved at Martha.

"Hello, you!" said the lady. "Am I late to the party?"

There was something about that lady. She looked messy, like a wild animal, Martha had thought. An animal turned into a human by an enchanted spell but who still had something of the forest clinging to her. Her eyes looked glazed and she was too skinny, and her smile pulled back fierce, revealing long teeth.

"Party?" Martha repeated.

"Isn't there a party? Balloons mean a party!"

Martha shook her head and ran. Ran as fast as she could. Ran up the lawn and into the house through the garage, and even when she was safe inside the Donnelleys' house, she had locked the door.

Her breath had burst forward, and she had stood there for a long time, panting, until she had collected herself enough to drop the mail in the living room and rejoin the other girls upstairs.

Now Martha closed her eyes and the knowledge sang in the back of her throat.

The lady is my secret, she thought. Mine to tell it when the time is right, and not a second before.

Leticia

Leticia couldn't help thinking that it was not all bad that Gray had disappeared. As long as nothing terrible had happened to her. As long as she came back soon. But right now it meant a break from the pink party. Topher was excited about it, too. After he rounded everyone back inside and into the kitchen, he handed out flashlights and spare batteries and ordered the girls to pair up.

"Each of you grab an official buddy, and stay together," he instructed. "Nobody else is getting lost on my watch."

"Guess I'll look with you," Martha whispered. When Topher had called her out of the dining room, she had slid up on Leticia's side.

Leticia did not answer. She switched her flashlight from its high to low beam. *Click, click.*

"If I can't look with you, I won't look at all," Martha said into Leticia's silence. Then: "I don't know what makes you think you can act like such a snot. You were being a jerk during Enchanted Castle, too. If you're mad at me, you should come out and say."

"Why would I be mad, Miss A-plus?" asked Leticia in a soft voice that sounded friendly.

She watched Martha's face go blank. "What are you talking about?"

"You know." *Click, click.* High, low. "That A plus you got on the earth science test. That grade is a lie, you cheater. After I told you that you couldn't copy me, you just switched seats and looked off Zoë's paper. I saw you do it. Now the proof is written next to your name in Ms. Calvillo's grade book. A plus."

"That test was a cinch." Martha covered her mouth as if to stifle a yawn, but her eyes were flinty. "It was stupid easy."

"Not *that* easy, considering." Leticia took a deep breath. "Considering I only got a B plus."

"Sucks to be you," Martha recited. She smirked. Then shrugged. Then she turned away from Leticia, sneaking back into the dining room.

Leticia unhooked her jacket from the pantry peg. Her throat was dry and her fingers were cold. Going up against Martha was hard. It was easier to be friends. Only three weekends ago, she had spent the night at Martha's house. It had been fun. Martha had filched her older sister Jane's diary to read to Leticia. Later that night, they'd phoned Ralph Dewey, a shy boy from Martha's church, and in spooky voices they had chanted,

"You are the son of the devil, Ralph Dewey! You are the son of the devil and you are going to hell!" while he squealed, "Who is this? What do you want from me?"

Then they had hung up and laughed until their stomachs hurt.

Later that night, Leticia had felt bad. The echo of Ralph Dewey's lonely voice would not leave her ear. And she was upset about Jane's diary, too, about knowing strange, private things personal to Martha's older sister.

Not that Martha cared, and Leticia was used to being on guard against Martha's tricks and pranks. Nobody was spared, not even Leticia herself. "Mar, do Leticia giving her oral report!" Caitlin had commanded the other day at lunch. The other girls had turned to Martha, their eyes gleaming expectantly. Obviously, they had heard this imitation before, Leticia realized, when she was not around. "Now, Teesh, don't be mad, it's *funny!*" Caitlin had coaxed. "Come on, do it for her, Mar!"

Martha had not needed to be asked twice. She had launched into a savage impression of Leticia presenting her social studies oral report. "There are, uh, ma-ny In-can sites through-out Per-u, uh, that have not yet been, uh, ex-ca-va-ted." Martha had it all down—the clogged, wobbling vowels, the gulped breaths, even the way Leticia fixed her eyes on the wall clock— as the other girls exploded with fits of giggling.

Of course, Leticia had to laugh along, pushing past the bead of anger that had lodged in her chest. Too harsh, Martha! she had wanted to protest. Public speaking took guts, even if she wasn't great at it. Now she had to be mocked for it, too?

But nobody was safe from Martha.

Leticia zipped up her jacket and stepped outside. The night spun a shiver through her. When she looked up, the stars twinkled and the moon looked full and soft as a cushion in the sky. Through the dining room window, Leticia watched Martha return to her seat and reach across the table for somebody else's goody bag. The back of her head looked small and lonely as an unpicked flower.

Leticia looked away. "Serena!" she called. She twirled her flashlight, which caught Serena's gingery hair like a sunlit wave in the light's beam. "Hey, come be my pair! Let's find Gray together, you and me!"

The search stopped being fun almost as soon as it started. For one thing, the temperature seemed to drop every minute. Also, anytime a pair of flashlights moved too far down the street, Topher called them back. Leticia stayed close to the pack. She watched as Mrs. Donnelley, Ty's hand gripped in hers, flitted from door to door, knocking, ringing bells, alerting everyone. Her phony voice: *"Hello! Sorry to bother you, but we're looking for a little girl. . . ."*

Soon a few of the neighbors had joined in to help. Over and over, in answer to their questions, Leticia described Gray.

Brown hair, chin length. Brown eyes. Wearing jeans with a navy and white snowflake sweater.

Nobody had seen her.

"Maybe she got stolen by a pack of wild dogs," Leticia joked.

"Woof! Woof! Pftew! This girl is too bony!" barked Caitlin.

"Don't say that," chided Mrs. Donnelley, overhearing them. She turned. "That's a terrible thing to say." Her features, normally pulled into this or that agreeable expression, all fell together into a hard glare. A glare aimed not at Caitlin, but Leticia.

Right there, that's Mrs. Donnelley's real face, Leticia thought. Uncertain, panicked.

What a phony.

Oh, sure, on the surface Mrs. Donnelley was nice enough. Usually her expression was a nearly perfect mask, pale eyes shiny and her smile stretched wide, right from the start. "Leticia, honey, what can I get you to *drink?*" "Leticia, honey, Caitlin says both of your parents are *lawyers!*" "Leticia, honey, I understand you were at *Rotterdam* last year?"

Always so extra-polite. Always with the *honey, honey.*

Phony, phony.

Last spring, Leticia had left Rotterdam Elementary as one of the most popular kids in her class. She had stood out as the girl with the quick jokes and throaty laugh, as the girl who could kick a soccer ball past any goalie, as the girl who could think up a million fads—like wearing gel stickers on the bottoms of her sneakers or gold Magic Markering her fingernails.

This past fall, when Leticia had started Fielding Academy, she'd stood out only as the black girl. Actually, the other black girl. But Daria Moore was ignored to the point where she seemed invisible. That was what Fielding girls did, Leticia's sister, Celeste, had told her. Fielding girls ignored. Ignoring was their specialty. Celeste had graduated from Fielding last year, and she knew everything.

Right away, Leticia had spotted the cool group. Martha Van Riet's group. As a whole, they were bigger than their parts. They joked the most. They laughed the hardest. They had the best time. They rubbed shoulders in an enchanted circle.

Martha was their leader, and the way in. Martha had a wide flat face like a freckled toad, and at first she did not smile at Leticia's jokes or care when Leticia laughed at hers. Martha did not seem to care about anything except being noticed. She was always sassing back at teachers or running in the hall or wearing nonregulation clothes with her uniform. Martha seemed fearless, and everyone was in awe of her.

It was during language arts class that Leticia made her move. She turned around in her chair, flipped Martha a Post-It note with a squiggly face drawn on it, and, with all the other girls listening, said, "Dare you to stick this note on Miss Bruce's butt."

Martha received the dare coldly. But she did it. Slapped on the note quick and perfect when Miss Bruce walked down the aisle, handing back homework.

That same day, right before the bell rang for history, Martha came back at her.

"Hey. Uh, Leticia. Dare you to pull down Mr. Wolferson's map of North America."

Mr. Wolferson was not in the classroom yet. Leticia acted fast, jumping up from her chair to rip it down with both hands and all her strength. Her stomach churned. The class chortled nervously. When Mr. Wolferson came in and demanded a culprit, nobody told because it was Martha Van Riet's dare.

They teamed up, Leticia and Martha. Dares were more fun to do together.

They made animal noises during chorus practice. They started a Tater Tots food fight during lunch. They faked injuries, limps, and spasms to annoy the gym teachers. They got detentions together.

Leticia slipped inside the loop of Martha's group. Soon after, Zoë nicknamed them the Lucky Seven. Inside the loop was everything in the world. Leticia felt home safe.

Only nothing is ever really safe, Leticia thought as she swept her flashlight back and forth like a lighthouse beam. She watched as Mrs. Donnelley and Ty crossed the street to ring another doorbell. Mrs. Donnelley was not really safe. She was too phony, and her home was hot and pink and bright and strange and slightly unwelcoming, no matter how many times Leticia had stayed over.

And Martha was not safe, either. Martha would do anything to get her way.

Suddenly, Serena squeezed her elbow. "Teesh, I'm scared!" she said. "It sounds weird. Listen."

Ty and Mrs. Donnelley and Topher and some of the neighbors were calling Gray's name. Gray's name was a single sound that did not stop.

Graaaaaaaaaaaaaaaaaaaaaaaaaaaaaaaaaaaaaaaaaaaaaaaaaay!

A lost, lonely sound, thought Leticia.

She hoped Gray was safe, wherever she was.

Leticia tucked Serena's hand more firmly into the crook of her elbow. "Nothing to be scared of," she said, though her thoughts skittered nervously as she took a long breath and then added her voice to the night.

Gray

All of Gray's favorite characters were brave and not like her. Brave Alice in Wonderland and Anne of Green Gables and Buffy the Vampire Slayer and Jo March and Heidi and Pippi and Nancy Drew and Becky Thatcher and Dorothy in and out of Oz. Brave, all of them. None of those girls would have liked Gray much. She was not the kind of girl Tom Sawyer or a stray dog would follow home. She was not the kind of girl who could summon that scrap of bravery that raised her just a tiny bit above the other girls. The feisty girl in the bittersweet adventure who was an inspiration, who made everybody clap and who gave everybody a bit of hope to cling to at the end.

No, Gray was not that kind of girl. Gray was a too-scared girl, and she knew it. Too scared of too many things. Of boys and stray dogs and the dark and bringing the wrong sleeping bag. She was scared of bigger things, too, of the smell of hospitals and of her mother maybe dying. She hoped that one day she would outgrow her fears, but so far, fear seemed to be sticking with her.

So when the strange lady who might be from Helping Hands offered her hand and ordered Gray to hurry up, and when she clamped her fingers around Gray's wrist and did not let go, Gray did not do anything brave. She decided to trust the lady because it was easier. If the lady had asked Gray to close her eyes and fall backward into her arms, Gray might have done that, too.

She tripped along at the lady's side. Out the sliding glass door into the freezing air and down the driveway and a left at the end of it, to where the lady's car was parked. An old car, too dark to see the color it truly was.

In the back of Gray's jumbled thoughts, one idea burned bright and kept her from turning and running. The lady did not look like someone from Helping Hands, but she did look like someone her mother might have met at the hospital.

She tested it. "You know Mom from the hospital?"

"Well," said the lady, "I don't like when people call it that."

"Are you sick?"

"The door's unlocked," the lady answered.

Gray touched the car door handle and looked around, hoping for a glimpse of a neighbor. But it was cold, too cold to be comfortably outside, and all of the brick or stone fortress-thick houses on Caitlin's street were set back from the road, for privacy. There was nobody to see or to be seen by. Gray did spy

Bumpo standing at the edge of the property because his electric collar did not permit him to escape his generous run of lawn. His head was cocked and quizzical.

"Can the dog come?" Gray asked. *Yes! Bumpo! It would be easy for me to take off his electric collar and say come on come on Bumpo come in the car for a ride! Just in case maybe things don't turn out all right maybe Bumpo saves the day! Because dogs do that yes sometimes on TV. Sometimes they do.*

"Don't be silly!" said the lady.

Oh, of course she was being silly. Gray opened the door and slid into the backseat of the car, and she buckled her seat belt, for Safety.

She would be gone and back before anyone noticed. She would get her sleeping bag and her mother would not have had to do all that driving, because she had sent in her place this odd lady, this "piece of work" who might be a friend or might not, who might be from Helping Hands or maybe not.

And even if her mother had not sent this lady, it would turn out okay, because the lady did not seem dangerous, in her glossy lipstick and feathery coat. She just looked a little bit confused. She would be happy to take Gray home and return her to the Donnelleys' before cake time.

Bumpo whined, then turned and trotted back to the house.

The car was rattling and noisy, as if it had swallowed a handful of coins. The lady took roads that Gray knew. But the ride was uncomfortable, unheated, and the tires slipped loose on the road. The lady drove as if she had only just learned, hunkered forward and her lower lip caught hard in her top teeth.

Out of the corner of her eye, Gray stared at the lady. Her face in the light-by-light reflection of the streetlamps was made up with eye shadow and rouge and a papery, sparkling powder smoothed over like a glittering fish skin to hold everything in place.

Maybe the lady was not one hundred percent real? Maybe she was a fairy, or an angel-ghost, and she was taking Gray on an adventure that would turn out to be a dream.

Gray touched a finger to the lady's feather-tufted coat collar.

"Don't do that!" the lady snapped. "Don't frighten me when I'm driving!"

Gray winced. That did not seem to be a very angel-y thing to say. "There's a price tag hanging off your coat sleeve," Gray said as she noticed it.

The lady shook her sleeve to see for herself, then bit it off, snapping the tag and little plastic tail in exactly the way Gray's mother told her not to because it damaged the fabric. The lady spit the tag and tail at the door. "Thanks," she said.

"What's your name?" asked Gray.

"Katrina." The woman thought for a moment, then added, "Just Katrina."

"I don't mind how fast you're driving," Gray said. "Since we have to get back to the Donnelleys' house soon. It's almost time for pizza and cake."

"I haven't driven a car in a while," said Katrina. "I liked driving, but it's not coming back easy. And I've been on the road so much today. All the way into town and around and around. When we get back, I'm going to take a nap."

"Back to my house, right?" When Katrina did not answer, Gray said, "I thought we were going to my house? If you want to take a nap on my bed, you can."

"My house first."

"Okay." Gray wished she didn't sound so scared. By now Nancy Drew would have found the important clue about Katrina, a clue to solve the mystery, and her story would have been called *The Clue in the Rattletrap Car.* Alice in Wonderland would have said "Curiouser and curiouser" without a trace of worry in her voice.

Driving down a dark road in a dark car with a strange lady seemed worse than curious. Gray decided she would try to imagine it in a friendlier and safer way, as an adventure.

Yes, that was how she would see it.

As an adventure!

Katrina lived at a turnoff at the end of a back road that Gray had never been down, but it was close to the same road that turned onto Knightworthy Avenue, which led to Fielding Academy. Gray had marked all these points in her mind.

Memory pebbles, she thought, which will lead my way back to Safety.

The house was small and paint-chipped, surrounded by shaggy pine trees peaked at the top like witch hats. One amber lightbulb burned above the stoop. Moths flew out of nowhere to fall against it.

Katrina got out of the car and slammed the door behind her. She seemed to have forgotten about Gray, who trotted behind. Gray was hungry. She made a plan. As soon as she was inside, she would use the phone first to call home, then the Donnelley house. She could give pretty good directions to this area, and people might be worried by now.

And after the phone calls, she would find something to eat.

She joined Katrina, who stood on the stoop, fumbling with her keys. They both stamped their feet to keep warm as Katrina drove key after key into the lock and jiggled the doorknob. The last key let them in.

Katrina clicked the lights and plowed ahead of Gray into a room that was small and cluttered with the kind of lightweight furniture most people used on their lawns or patios. It was even messy like a patio, littered with soda cans and magazines and ashtrays and clear plastic glasses and stacks of fast-food napkins.

"I need to make a phone call," Gray said. "Everyone is allowed a phone call. Isn't that some kind of rule of the law?"

"The phone is turned off, I guess the bill wasn't paid," said Katrina. "Do you want to watch television?" She pointed to a television positioned on a table against the far wall. It was square and old-fashioned, with bunny-eared antennae tips padded in aluminum foil.

"No," Gray answered. She looked around for a telephone. Maybe Katrina was lying? When she did not see a telephone anywhere, a new, raw nervousness hummed in her throat and ears. Her eyes pricked with the tears that never were too far away. "I made a mistake," she admitted out loud, "and I want to go home. You said you would take me home."

"Oh. But I don't know where you live."

"Well, *I* do," said Gray. "And you know where Caitlin lives. We just came from there. Actually, I want to go back to Caitlin's birthday party. I'm missing all the fun. I'm missing . . . things."

Katrina seemed to think about it. Under the stark overhead light, Gray noticed that her eyes looked feverish, a thin border of dark blue nearly drowned by animal-black pupils. "Let's wait until Drew comes home," Katrina said. "I'm low on gas, and I'm not feeling good enough to drive anyone anywhere."

"You have to bring me home or back to the Donnelleys' house. Now," Gray insisted. "Please, I mean. I have twenty-eight dollars in my savings account. I'll write you a note giving it all to you. You can buy a lot of gas with that money. As long as you take me away."

"Well, listen to you, thinking you can order me around!" Katrina's laugh was harsh. "I already took you away! Now I'm spent. I should lie down." She pulled at the handkerchief. The ropy brown hair had been attached to it, and now it all came off in a heap, revealing Katrina's real hair, which was extremely short and prickly pale as a spring peach.

So it was true, after all! Katrina was sick. She had been in the hospital. Gray softened. "Are you having chemotherapy?" she asked politely.

Absently, Katrina dabbed a finger at her scalp. "A little nap," she said. "A night nap."

Gray continued, "My mother is sick. She got a wig last year, when she was having chemotherapy, but she's better now. Her real hair has grown back in. My brother wore the wig for Halloween. He sprayed it with glitter and was a rock star."

"I'm better, too," said Katrina. "That's what Drew said. That's why he took me away before I could have my party. But he said we'd have another party." She smiled. When she smiled, she appeared childlike, younger even than Robby. "Don't worry. Drew will come back soon."

"You don't understand, they'll be wondering . . ." But Katrina was finished with Gray. She turned and slipped down the short hall and disappeared behind a door.

Then Gray searched the front room inch by inch until she discovered a telephone under the couch. There was no dial tone. She plugged the phone into another outlet, double-checking, before she gave up and slid the phone back under the couch where she'd found it.

There was not a lot to the rest of the house. Gray walked through it carefully, looking for clues. Through the cracked-open bedroom door, she saw Katrina sprawled facedown and motionless on a bare twin frame. Aside from the bed, there was a blowup chair, the type used in a swimming pool, with a palm tree design and a drink holder sunk into its arm. The chair was half deflated, sagging sideways as if it, too, were asleep. The door next to the bedroom revealed a bathroom. In the back of the house was a skinny wedge of kitchen.

Retracing her steps, Gray opened the door to the hall closet to find it filled with winter coats and boots and, in the corner, a tiny dead brown mouse that had been long caught and crushed in a spring trap. Gray gasped—she had never seen a dead mouse before, and she would not brave inspecting this one. *Little lump his neck is squished oh so mean those mean traps little paw poor poor mousey.* She slammed the door. Shivering, she ran back to the couch, where she sat, pulling at the blanket draped over its back, and then wrapping it around her shoulders.

She was cold. She had left the Donnelley house without her coat.

They would probably be calling her name, searching for her inside and outside. It had been a while since she left. Caitlin would be angry. Mrs. Donnelley might be upset, too. She did not like for things to go wrong and to interfere with her perfect plans.

Gray hated to think of Mrs. Donnelley being upset, and knowing that she was the reason for it. Dumb, oh, this was so dumb, to have convinced herself that Katrina was from Helping Hands! When in the back of her mind, she had known all along. . . . And it was her mother's fault! If her mother hadn't gotten sick, there wouldn't be such a thing as Helping Hands. If her mother wasn't sick, she would not make mistakes about which sleeping bag.

Now here I am stuck here in this little lonely bad house without my sleeping bag and probably I missed the cake too.

She tried to find something cheerful in her mind to tug on to, a festive thought, like one of Caitlin's pink balloons, but a blur of new fears batted at her. She wanted to scream. A scream began thickly in her stomach and expanded, filling her lungs, her toes and fingertips. She pressed her knuckles against her mouth. Jumped up from the couch and walked outside in case she had to release it.

The night was huge and black, but no worse than the dark thoughts that swept in and out of her as she tried to imagine everything that might be lurking. Gray hopped off the stoop and took a few faltering steps. As far as she could see—which was not far, because of the trees—was nothing. Without sight of the road, the house seemed sunk too deep in the woods, like the gingerbread house in "Hansel and Gretel" or the lone cottage of the Seven Dwarfs.

An adventure might be even better than Caitlin's party. After all, it was an escape from the Donnelleys' loud, warm house and boring Enchanted Castle. It was an escape from food that looked better than it tasted. Best, Gray escaped faking happiness when Caitlin opened Gray's present, a *Make It Yourself!* beadwork kit that Gray herself desired so badly, she had considered keeping it and giving Caitlin an unopened package of bath salts. One of those "get well soon" gifts people were always foisting on her mother.

Caitlin already had everything, anyway. She'd bead one necklace and shove the kit on the top shelf space of her closet on top of her *Material Girl* fabric-patching kit and *Jamboree Gems* glass-polishing kit.

"I am not in any danger." Gray spoke out loud. "I can always run off into the woods and then follow the road to Fielding. Even if it took me until morning, by then maybe the police will be looking for me. So. I know where I am. I know where I am."

The sound of her voice and the truth of her words eased her mind. She went back into the house. The next plan would be to keep calm, to watch television, and to wait for Katrina's friend Drew, whoever he was.

Whoever he is he will know what to do.

Another quick check in the bedroom showed that Katrina must have moved a bit, because now her pretty coat was crumpled in a heap on the floor.

"Katrina?" called Gray softly.

Katrina's breathing was deeper, heavier than regular napping. It reminded Gray of the way her mother slept, and seemed stronger proof that Katrina and her mother were linked. Yes, Katrina was sick, and the medication was affecting her abilities.

"Katrina?" she called again.

No answer. Gray retreated into the living room and turned on the television.

The remote control was touchy, none of the channels came in well, and there was no cable. Her hunger was beginning to make her feel light-headed. She wished she had taken some more grapes. She pressed her head against the dark window glass.

What would Heidi do? What would Gretel do? What would Pippi do? They understood the outdoors and how to navigate it using their own wits.

Think. Think.

Although her heartbeat ticked too quickly, Gray was surprised by her calm. She could feel the flame of fear inside her, yes, but it was not a wildfire, she was not burning up, she had not been engulfed. Not yet, anyway.

Zoë

Zoë would find Gray. She would find her and her picture would be in the newspaper. She would be the hero. She would be the winner.

Zoë's picture had been in the local paper twice before.

Once for the Fielding Academy Science Fair, where she had won second prize for a pinball machine she had constructed using thin pipes that played a tune depending on how you hit the ball. Only it didn't work exactly because no tune played, just haphazard ping—ping—ping notes. So stupid! Why hadn't she done an important project about arthritis, like Natalie Brady, who won first prize?

The second picture was for the Maple Creek Water Club Intermediate Swimming Championships. Zoë had won first place for breaststroke, that was good, but the photograph taken was of Zoë in her bathing suit. Horrible! Her face and her name, paired with the word *breast*, pinned up in the school's front lobby on the "Regional News and Events" bulletin board.

When the others saw that picture, they'd made fun of her. "Yoo-hoo! Look at you, Zoë!" Serena had teased. "What's next? The *Sports Illustrated* calendar?"

"Zoë should swim breastless stroke," added Caitlin.

Martha had looked and said, simply, "Dork."

Zoë had never thought about how she actually *looked* as a swimmer until that picture. Her parents had always told Zoë that she was "attractive," with her dark, curly Atacropolis hair and her square chin, and she had blindly believed it. Stupid! She had ripped down the newspaper clipping to stare at it in the privacy of her own room, a blood-rush of shame in her cheeks, wondering if her bangs fell crooked or if there was something funny about her chin. And of course hating her non-breasts, squashed flatter under her swimming suit.

If Zoë found Gray tonight, she would get another chance, and a better photo in the paper. This time, it would be perfect. "Local Girl Saves School Pal." Her bangs styled just right and her chin tucked, with her arm hooked confidently around Gray's shoulder. No stupid breastless bathing suit. No second place.

Just last week, Zoë's brother, Shelton, had been quoted in *The Wall Street Journal* because he knew every single thing there was to know about business technology. "Your son, Shelton, is a genius," people often said to her parents.

"Zoë's no lightweight," her father would answer.

"Zoë's quite bright herself," her mother would refrain.

They never said she was a genius, though.

If she found Gray, then Zoë figured she would be better than a genius. She would be a psychic. Because in the interview next to the picture of them, Zoë would be quoted explaining how a shivery feeling came over her, how an electric black-and-white picture *of exactly where Gray was* had zapped into her head and she knew.

"I'll find you, Gray," whispered Zoë to the night.

She tore down the street. They were supposed to stay in groups, but the others were no help because they didn't care enough about winning.

The night was cold, too cold to be out for the fun of it.

Why would Gray have left the nice, safe house?

Zoë inhaled deep into the bottom of her lungs and called Gray's name. The sound went on and on like a bell.

I am superhuman, Zoë thought. My powers are greater than the others. I will get a supernatural picture of Gray in my head. It will direct me to the pothole where Gray tripped and broke her leg. It will direct me right to the side of the road where Gray got hit—but not too bad—by a car.

Please let me be the one to find you, Gray.

She hoped Gray was okay, wherever she was. Maybe she had run away on purpose. Maybe she was sick of Caitlin and the Lucky Seven and having to hide in the bathroom when she was sad. Maybe she was tired of pretending that she was the same sweet, easygoing, no-problems-here Gray from back in fifth grade, before her mother got sick. Maybe, if Zoë found her first, Gray would confess all these things and Zoë would not tell the others like last time.

Because this time, she would protect Gray against Martha's mean jokes and Caitlin's bored face. Yes, yes, she could do that.

Zoë widened her eyes until they hurt. She thought she might be able to see in the dark. Tonight her hearing seemed animal-sharp. She had watched plenty of TV shows about mystics and psychics and fortune-tellers. The senses were everything.

"I found Gray because people in my family have the Sight," she would tell everyone at lunch on Monday. "I guess I do, too. It's no big deal. I was born to it."

She would become a local legend. Wouldn't her parents be proud! And wouldn't Shelton, Mr. Business Technology, be jealous! Though of course not to her face. To her face Shelton would have to praise her.

Zoë ran on and on, her mind open and waiting to receive the Sight.

"I'll find you, Gray," she whispered. "I promise."

Martha

The grandfather clock in the front hall chimed seven times.

Martha had settled on the bottom step of the staircase. She sat very still and listened to the endless shouting for Gray across and up and down the street.

She wondered if Gray was safe or in danger.

In danger, she bet, with a tug of envy. Wherever Gray was and whatever she was doing, Martha bet that it was more exciting than anything happening in this house.

Occasionally someone came inside, up or down the stairs, past Martha. Once, as Mrs. Donnelley swept by, the cold of the outdoors on her body, she said, "That's right, you stay there, Martha. In case Gray comes through the front door. You call for me right away. I'm just outside. Tell Mr. Donnelley, too, when he comes down. I'm just outside."

Mrs. Donnelley did not want to think that Martha simply had decided not to look for Gray. Which she had. Frankly, she did not feel like looking for anything, and her stomach ached from chocolate. Besides, it only would have been fun to search for Gray with Leticia, and Leticia was acting strange tonight. Martha wished she would snap out of it. Since when did Leticia care so much about stupid school stuff?

As the sound of chiming fell away, the Donnelleys' dog, Bumpo, began to bark outside.

"Bumpo! Quiet, Bumpo!"

"Does he see anything?"

"I think he's barking at a squirrel."

"Are you sure?"

Bumpo kept barking. *Wolf wolf wolf! Rough rough rough!*

Too late, Bumpo, thought Martha. You think you're such a good watchdog! Why weren't you watching Mouse?

Martha listened to the distant rush of water through the pipes as Mr. Donnelley showered. A long shower, considering that Gray was missing and Mr. Donnelley said he would be the one to take charge. Maybe he was taking his time on purpose, Martha thought, to scare Mrs. Donnelley. To show her that he was the one making the decisions, however slow or fast he needed. To show her that she had messed up bad.

She watched the clock tick past eleven more minutes before Mr. Donnelley thudded downstairs. Damp, red-faced, and changed into an ugly tan-striped tracksuit. He plodded past Martha and into the dining room, his cell phone in hand, talking to himself.

"The mail, the mail. What the . . . ? Did we not get mail today?" He was peering into an empty basket on the console. He was standing so close to Martha that she could have stepped on his slippered foot.

"There." From her perch on the first step, Martha leaned forward and pointed across the hall to the coffee table in the darkened living room.

That's where the mail got dropped in her house.

Mr. Donnelley frowned as he noticed Martha. He lumbered into the living room. Martha watched him snatch up the stack of mail, cross the hall back into the dining room, and drop the whole bundle in the console's mail basket. Then he took all the mail out again to read, proving his point to nobody.

Picky, picky, thought Martha. That's the Donnelleys. Him *and* her. Maybe that's what made them marry each other. Or maybe one turned picky to copycat the other.

Mr. Donnelley ripped open envelopes and hardly read their contents. Soon, he had discarded the whole mess in the mail basket.

"Yes, I'm here!" he barked into the phone. "I've been holding for over three minutes. Hope this doesn't indicate how you guys handle emergencies!" There was grit in his voice. Mr. Donnelley was used to getting things done. Martha bet he was a mean dad or boss when he got angry. "I'd like to report a child who might be missing. Description? Um, stay right there. Let me put my wife on the line."

When the two police arrived in their squad car, the Donnelley house became a public place of banging doors, of heavy footsteps, of deep adult voices asking questions, of walkie-talkie static and blue lights swirling.

The police, Officer Mustache and Officer Bird Eyes, ordered the girls to come inside—"Too dangerous!"—and they asked them all the same things.

Who had seen Gray last?

Approximately when was Gray seen last?

What was the last thing Gray said?

Where did Gray say she was going?

Zoë talked the most, but Ty had the most answers. He said Gray had left the family room to get some juice the same minute the car Fiori Dulce passed Renata in the Daytona 500.

"It's a rerun, but we can still pinpoint that time," said Officer Bird Eyes, making a note in her book.

Martha's own secret squeezed her stomach. Should she tell the police about that lady by the mailbox? No, no, not now. The right moment would come. Besides, it was fun to have a secret. It was fun to hold her secret like a chocolate heart melting in her mouth.

"Look, guns!" said Leticia, pointing to the holsters as the officers went upstairs to talk to Mr. and Mrs. Donnelley privately, in the den.

"My dad owns a gun," Serena admitted softly.

"Mine, too," lied Martha, trying to imagine her bookworm father with a gun dangling from his soft hand.

"Rugrats, listen up," said Topher. "Cops say you have to stay put and all together. So we're gonna camp out here in the dining room. You leave only with special permission, and only for, like, the bathroom. Got it? 'Cause we don't know if there's, y'know, someone . . ." His eyes darted to the window, to the parked police car alive with light and scratchy sound.

"Gray is ruining my party!" Caitlin burst out. "I'm sick of looking for her and thinking about her!"

"Me, too," added Kristy.

"Wow. If your friend got, like, *hit* by a *bus* and is lying in some, like, *hospital* room, *unconscious* and *bleeding*," Topher answered, "then I personally will go sit beside her bed and wait for her to wake up. So that I can be the first one to tell her how *you guys* said she, like, *ruined* your party. Some friends *you* are. *Brats*, more like. Now who wants pizza? Plain or pepperoni?" He pointed to Leticia. "Plain or pepperoni? Let's go!"

"I'm lactose intolerant," said Leticia. She had not looked at Martha once since she had come inside. Not once. Leticia was being a pain. A real fun-wrecker, and all over such a tiny thing as cheating.

"The pizza's cold," said Serena.

"I'm not hungry," added Zoë.

Martha said, "Lemonade and pepperoni."

Topher snapped his fingers and pointed at her in a way that

made Martha blush. "Take an example from this kid. One lemonade, one slice of pepperoni, coming up. If it's too cold, give it to me and I'll stick in it the microwave."

Girls glanced uncertainly at Martha and then began to sit down, spreading their laps with pink napkins as Topher opened the pizza boxes on the sideboard. He used a spatula to carry and slide the first piece onto Martha's plate. He poured her lemonade. Martha said thank you and took a huge bite to show the rest of them how easy it was.

One by one, the other girls asked for orange, grape, or lemonade. For plain or pepperoni. Leticia peeled cheese off her slice without a word. Nobody said that the pizza was too cold, although it was.

Topher moved around them like a hasty waiter, the type Martha's parents would complain about. He removed Gray's place setting, slapping the paper cup and plate on the sideboard.

When Mrs. Donnelley returned to the dining room, Martha could tell she had been crying. Her eyes had that salted look. With a wobbling arm, she picked up the grape soda bottle, found an empty pink cup, and aimed.

"The police say that Gray has probably wandered off on her own adventure and will be back soon," said Mrs. Donnelley, rocking the bottle up and down so that the liquid tipped out in small spurts. "The one officer said it happens all the time! It's only been maybe two hours at the most. Silly girl! I don't know what I'll do when I see her again. Hug her very tight, I guess!

Very tight! Who wanted this cup of grape soda? Oops, maybe I poured it for myself!"

She laughed and took a sip. Mrs. Donnelley thought she had them fooled, but she didn't fool Martha, even as she forced the birthday party to continue.

"Cake time!" she sang.

She carried out Caitlin's candlelit pink cake and started the girls singing "Happy Birthday" and she didn't let Caitlin blow out the candles because Caitlin was just getting over a cold and nobody wanted germs, right, girls? Then she returned the cake to the pantry for Topher to cut and serve, and she set the tray of presents from the sideboard in front of Caitlin.

"Open mine! Open mine!" the other girls begged.

Martha did not want Caitlin to open hers. She squeezed out of her seat and trailed Mrs. Donnelley back into the pantry.

"Stan Rosenfeld works in the city, I just got hold of him and he's on his way," Martha overheard Mrs. Donnelley say in a low voice to Topher. "He thinks Lenora took Robby to an early movie and dinner, so nobody's at the Rosenfelds' house right now. He's going to get a neighbor over in the event Gray shows up there. Oh, dear lord, if something happened to that child, nobody will ever forgive . . ."

Mrs. Donnelley bumped against Martha as she swung around the corner, a pink plate of pink cake in each hand. She blinked. "Martha, what are you doing in here? Go sit down," she chided. "It's almost time for presents."

Martha scowled. Her mother had bought Caitlin's birthday present, and it was sort of stupid. A green velvet beret and matching mittens. But her mother preferred practical gifts to toys, and she had said it was either the beret-and-mittens set or a giant leather-bound *Complete Works of Shakespeare.*

"Mom! That's, like, a present that a teacher would give!" Martha had protested.

"Oh, Martha. If your sister Jane were as critical as you, I'd be at my wit's end." Her mother had flopped her pocketbook on the counter. "Let's take the hat set, then. It's absolutely adorable and it's on sale. End of story."

At the time, Martha had been relieved that her mother had not tried to push the Shakespeare book. But the hat-and-mittens set was not a good present, either.

Right this very moment, it seemed especially bad. Totally *unc.* And with Leticia acting all nasty tonight, Martha knew there was a chance she might get teased for it. Martha preferred to be the tease-r, not the other way around.

She waited until Mrs. Donnelley went upstairs to join Mr. Donnelley and the police. Caitlin had just opened Kristy Kiss-up's gift, three CDs and a bottle of SPF 30 glitter sunscreen.

The other girls ooohed, how expensive, how nice!

Topher's cell phone rang and he stepped into the kitchen to take the call in private.

Martha slipped out of her seat and followed him.

I have to go to the bathroom, she mouthed.

Topher put his hand on the mouthpiece. "Use the one down here."

She nodded, then left swiftly through the pantry and raced upstairs. She sneaked past the den, pausing a moment to listen in on what was being said behind the closed door. In voices soft and overlapping, the police and Mr. and Mrs. Donnelley were talking about assembling a search party, about who else to notify, about what to do and what not to do.

". . . keep the little girls together until their parents come for them," said one of the officers.

"Yes, yes. Topher has it under control," squeaked Mrs. Donnelley.

They were being sent home? Tonight? Ha ha ha. Some party. Oh, this would be a good one to hold over Caitlin. How her birthday party was the worst one of the year. Martha smiled to herself and took a lively hop hop hop down the hall.

The Donnelley house was boring for exploring. It did not have secrets. The lights burned too high for shadows and the wastepaper baskets were empty. Inside every closet that Martha opened, the hangers faced the same way and the clothes hung straight and unwrinkled.

In the master bedroom, Martha discovered that Mrs. Donnelley's closet was sorted by color. Pale to dark, then prints, with hatboxes on top and a partitioned shelf to house each pair of shoes. Martha rearranged a few pairs with their wrong mates.

Mr. Donnelley's closet had plenty more ugly tracksuits. Maybe he thought tracksuits made him look young and athletic, and disguised the fact that he was too old for Mrs. Donnelley? Nice try, thought Martha. He looked especially old in their wedding picture, compared with Mrs. Donnelley, whose hair was like black silk while he had about three strands left. Gross. Why had Mrs. Donnelley picked him?

She placed the wedding picture facedown on the nightstand.

It was inside the cedar chest at the foot of the Donnelleys' bed, underneath the neatly folded squares of sweaters, that Martha found her treasure. A cellophane package of mothballs, delicate as spun sugar candies.

Aha!

She knew mothballs were seriously poisonous. One of Martha's first memories was of her mother uncurling her fingers to pry out a mothball like a pearl from its shell. Then cuffing both Martha's hands under the running faucet.

"Never, ever! Where is your sense, Martha?"

Martha ripped out a Kleenex from Mrs. Donnelley's bedside table, then she opened the package. The sweet, acrid smell burst into the air. Making pincers of her fingers, she pronged and dropped a single mothball into the Kleenex, then folded it neatly. Stole down the hall into Caitlin's room, where she tucked the packet in the zip pocket of her carryall bag.

She smiled as she zipped her bag. It was fun to sneak around, mess with things, claim tiny souvenirs. She liked to think of the dopey Donnelleys puzzling over the turned-over wedding picture, the mismatched shoes, and the ripped cellophane package.

Where is your sense, Martha?

Her parents both liked sense, and so did her big sister, Jane. All they did was read, read, read. They never did anything. It was always up to Martha to do the fun things, to shake things up and flip them upside down, even if it meant getting into trouble. Martha was usually willing to risk trouble over sense. That's why she was the head of the Lucky Seven.

In Caitlin's bathroom, Martha scrubbed the smell of stinky mothballs from her hands. Then she sat on the bath mat and waited until she was sure that her present was unwrapped and done with.

Leticia

"Martha's not here because she got you a lick present."

Leticia was guessing, but she bet it was true. Mrs. Van Riet was a mom who purchased practical gifts. Mrs. Van Riet was practical to a fault, and completely preoccupied with health. Whenever Leticia stayed over at Martha's, there was always a salad plus a vegetable and boring juice Popsicles for dessert. Mrs. Van Riet was also the only mother Leticia knew who had taped little *x*es on the rug to show how far away you were supposed to sit from the television. Mr. Van Riet was no better, either, always layering Martha against the cold and telling her about how scientific studies proved that sunlight and dyed food were potentially deadly.

"Quick, open it!" Leticia said. She thumped her fist on the table.

"Open it!"

"Open it!"

"Open it!"

Caitlin clawed at the wrapping paper.

"What is it? What did she give you?" Leticia craned forward.

With the tips of her fingers, Caitlin held up a green velvet beret and a pair of matching mittens attached by a string.

"Mittens!" Exaggeratedly, Leticia slapped a hand over her mouth.

Serena laughed. "Who wears mittens, right?" she asked softly, looking over at Leticia and shaking back her hair.

"God, that is so cheap," whispered Kristy, sliding her eyes at Caitlin. "That must have cost the least amount of any of our presents."

"No kidding." Zoë's voice was quiet, too. Leticia knew that it was because nobody wanted to risk the chance of Martha over-hearing.

The dare rushed through her and made her talk loud. "Hey, you guys, let's call Martha *Meow*," she suggested. "You know, like, because of the three little kittens who lost their mittens?"

The others looked at Leticia and giggled and then looked around at one another. Rarely did they gang up on Martha. Usually they spent their time trying not to land on the wrong end of one of Martha's jokes.

"All of us have to call her that, or it won't work," coaxed Leticia. "C'mon. It'll be funny."

Kristy picked up the mittens. "Meow, meow, meow," she said. "I can do a good meow, I don't even move my lips and I sound just like a cat, listen."

Through tensed, slightly parted lips, she made tiny mewing noises, and the others agreed she sounded exactly, completely like a cat.

"You should do that when Martha's around," said Leticia. "You're so good at it. Nobody can even tell it's you. I *dare* you."

Kristy looked nervous.

"I double-dare you," said Caitlin.

That did it. Kristy agreed with a nod.

Martha came back into the dining room.

"Hey, where've you been, *Meow?*" quipped Leticia. Stifled laughter sounded around the table.

Martha gave Leticia a look. Leticia returned it, dead-on, although her heart tripped fast and frightened. She had never played a trick on Martha before.

Until now. Waves of angry thought chopped at her. How could Ms. Calvillo be so blind? Martha never, ever put effort into science class. An A plus was such obvious cheating! Leticia set her chin and tried not to let her face betray her. She wondered why she cared so much. Maybe it was because she had studied so hard and only got a B plus. Or maybe she was just sick of Martha, sick of her traitor's jokes, sick of laughing along.

"Kiddos!" barked Topher, clapping his hands as he reentered through the kitchen. "Clear your plates. Grown-ups are taking over the main floor, and we're going downstairs to watch movies. But first, everyone into the kitchen to help Caitlin's mom call your parents."

"Why are we calling parents?" asked Caitlin. "Is my party ending? Gray is coming back soon, I know it. My party shouldn't end just because Gray left for a little while!"

"My party shouldn't end!" Ty mimicked in a squeaky voice.

"You're dead!" Caitlin grabbed him from behind and they both crashed to the floor, scratching and yanking at each other. Leticia watched. She was glad she had an older sister instead of a little brother.

"Kitchen, kitchen," Topher ordered. Then he began pulling at Caitlin and Ty. "Can't we call peace between you two for one lousy second?" he growled as he heaved them apart.

Leticia jumped up from her seat and herded through the door into the kitchen with the others. She took care to keep away from Martha.

The kitchen was crowded with the unfamiliar faces of the Donnelleys' neighbors. From outside came voices, people joining forces to organize in small search parties. Scouting, shouting, talking on phones, counting off into car caravans, sounding off opinions that rattled in Leticia's ears—"What could have happened to her?" "Oh, please! Nothing, *nothing* bad ever happens in this neighborhood." "She could have gone . . .

where would she have gone?" "And we're sure they've checked the whole house?" "The basement? Everywhere? Everywhere?"

Most parents were not available. Mrs. Donnelley kept leaving messages.

Leticia's mom and dad were in Key West at a conference until Sunday. Leticia listened to Mrs. Donnelley explain the situation to her family's housekeeper, Mrs. Grange. "Leticia is perfectly welcome to stay until tomorrow, and then I'll take her home," said Mrs. Donnelley in her best phony hostess voice. "But we want to notify everyone of the . . . situation."

Leticia knew she was staying because Mrs. Grange did not know how to drive.

Kristy's mom was out to dinner with her boyfriend.

Martha's parents were out of state, at a bed-and-breakfast. Leticia heard Martha tell Mrs. Donnelley that she did not know the name of it. Leticia had a hunch this was a lie, but Mrs. Donnelley was too upset and distracted to question her.

Zoë's mom was playing violin with the city orchestra tonight. Her dad was in the audience with his cell phone turned off.

Serena's parents were home. They said they would be right over.

Topher counted heads like duck-duck-goose. Then he led the girls and Ty from the kitchen back downstairs to the family room.

"It's still my birthday party, and I still pick *Titanic*," squawked Caitlin, spreading her arms across the television screen as if to protect it from another choice of movie. "Topher, it's in the rack. Will you put it on?"

Ty made two thumbs down and started to boo. Topher swatted him. "Yo, it's still your sister's night tonight, Ty, so cool your jets."

Topher stood in front of them, spinning the *Titanic* disk on his finger. He had a way of doing things in a careless, collegeish way. All at once, Leticia was overwhelmed with a sharp, aching wish to see her sister. A desire to run as fast as she could out of the Donnelleys' house, across three states, straight to Celeste's campus and dormitory and into the security of her arms. Too much about tonight was out of place. Celeste would know how to make things right again.

"Here's the rules," Topher said. "Pay attention 'cause it's just three words. Everybody Stay Put." Topher's eyes moved to Ty. "And the men are gonna watch this movie and like it. It's that or bed."

"Aww . . ." Ty rolled onto the floor and propped his chin in his elbows.

Titanic was so boring, especially since Leticia had seen it a thousand times. She suppressed a sigh as she curled up in the armchair and opened her goody bag. Other girls dropped onto the couch or carpet. Bumpo's eyes followed Leticia's fingers as she poked a chocolate into her mouth. She took out another chocolate and stealthily dropped it to the rug. Bumpo gulped it down happily.

"*Titanic* is crap," Martha muttered, lifting her head from where she was stretched under the coffee table.

Leticia leaned forward. "Wow, I can't believe you said that!" she exclaimed. "Criticizing Caitlin's favorite movie on her birthday. Sheez!"

"Yeah, Mar," Serena agreed, flipping her hair. "What's your problem?"

Martha scowled. "Sor-ry. But at least I'm not trying to make my friend's dog sick by feeding him chocolate. You might as well give him poison, Leticia. Don't you know anything about dogs? Chocolate is potentially deadly to canines." She sounded just like her father, Leticia thought.

But Caitlin turned and shot Leticia a look of exasperation. "Yeah, Martha's right. Don't feed Bumpo chocolate," she said, while Ty jumped up and began to pry open Bumpo's jaws.

"He already ate it," Ty announced.

"Nice going, Leticia," said Martha.

"I didn't mean to," Leticia mumbled, careful to avoid Martha's eyes and the tiny gleam of triumph she knew would be shining in them.

Topher's cell phone rang. He picked it up and edged to the back of the room, sliding into the beanbag chair. Leticia listened.

"Yo, dude! Uh-uh. Not a trace, and we're going on, like, three hours. Aw, dude, I can't come *out*. We got cops here!" Topher's whisper cracked with excitement.

The movie's sound was turned up loud, but voices made a constant static above. Leticia could hear that Mrs. Rosenfeld had arrived with Gray's little brother, Robby. Then she thought she heard Mr. Rosenfeld's voice, too, along with the more distant scratch of police shortwaves.

We are like the Enchanted Castle princesses, thought Leticia. We are trapped here in the dungeon while real things in the real world are spinning all around us.

A few minutes later, Serena's parents arrived, chattering, jostling down the stairs behind Mrs. Donnelley, and making so much fuss that Caitlin had to press PAUSE.

Serena stumbled to her feet, reluctant. "I don't wanna . . ." she began. But Mr. Hodgson pulled her up in his arms while Mrs. Hodgson touched Serena's nose, her cheeks, her hair, to reassure herself that all the princess pieces of lovely Serena were here.

They were overprotective, those Hodgsons, half-crazy with parent love. Like that time when Serena fell in gymnastics competition, Leticia remembered, how they swept in from the audience and scooped her up and away like she was made out of stars and glass.

Her own mom and dad were different. They had raised Celeste and Leticia to be independent. They weighed and balanced and related everything back to The Law, to Ethics and Conduct and Responsibility. "Figure it out," Leticia's mom liked to say. "It's your life. You live with your decisions, and you should be prepared to defend them."

The Hodgsons held a parent net to catch Serena every time. Now Leticia watched them cling to her. Then Mrs. Hodgson turned to Mrs. Donnelley. "It's *late*. Shouldn't the girls be in bed? Some are staying the night, isn't that correct?"

"Yes, yes, yes." Mrs. Donnelley sounded defeated. Her mother power was gone since she had lost Gray. She was not being who she liked to be—a show-off perfect mother. A mother who said, "Caitlin, you really need a hair trim!" or "Caitlin, let's get you some new sneakers because your other ones are absolutely, positively *shot*."

Ha, ha, thought Leticia.

After Mrs. Donnelley and the Hodgsons went upstairs, Zoë said, "Maybe the Hodgsons came because they want to take Serena far away and safe from the kidnapper. Like what happened to that other girl. Remember that story in the newspapers?"

"There's no kidnapper! Shut up!" Caitlin threw a pillow at Zoë's head.

"I was only thinking out loud," said Zoë.

"Yeah, but don't say stuff like that, Zoë. Just because Gray is missing *temporarily* doesn't mean that poor Caitlin's birthday

party should be ruined." Kristy's voice was stern. "She'll probably be back any minute."

"Thanks, Kristy," said Caitlin in a sad little voice.

"That kidnapper was a man, though," said Martha. "Right,
Zoë?" Leticia thought she detected worry or something like it in
Martha's voice.

"Yeah, yeah, that's right. Remember?" Zoë sat up. "It was all
over the news a while back, every channel, my mom was talking about it all the time, that horrible scary story about that
girl—"

"Stop, Zoë, I swear, or I'll get nightmares!" yelled Caitlin.

"Hey, kids, lower your voices, how about?" called Topher
from where he was, on another phone call.

"C'mon, everyone stop talking and play the movie." Leticia
did not want to think about kidnappers, or worse. She thumped
her fist like a gavel. "It's just getting good. It's about to start
sinking."

The room hushed. Caitlin pressed PLAY and raised the vol-
ume.

From somewhere in the room came the sound of a cat
meow.

"Did you hear that?" asked Martha after a moment.

Nobody answered.

"It sounds like a cat!"

Nobody said a word.

"Gee, you're all so funny, I forgot to laugh," said Martha with a yawn.

Kristy raised her mouth and eyebrows and looked over at Leticia, who smiled.

It was working. It was really working.

They were following Leticia. They were playing her game. Ignore-Martha-till-she-cries.

Only Martha never cried, did she?

Gray

The voice woke her.

"Kathy!" he said. "Kat. Get out here! Who is that kid?"

Gray opened her eyes to see a man standing in the middle of the room. From outside, she heard the rumble of a car driving away too fast.

Kathy, Kat. That was Katrina.

The man, who must be Drew, was not much older than Topher. He was small, heavy-boned, and fattish around his middle. Not as nice-looking as Topher. No, not at all, with that bumpy pink skin and those gluey, oyster-blue eyes. His hair straggled over his ears and a plum-colored tattoo of a swan marked the upper half of one of his arms. Then Gray saw it was a birthmark.

In a fairy tale, Drew would not have been the handsome prince, but he might have been the tailor's apprentice or the cook's apprentice. The jolly, foolish man who somewhere along the way has helped the unlucky princess. Who, as a reward at the end of the story, gets to work at the palace.

Drew did not look very jolly right now. He looked angry and confused.

Katrina shuffled from the bedroom as Gray sat up and wiped some drool from her cheek.

Drew turned. "Kat?" he drawled. "Who's the girl, Kat?"

"My name is Gray Rosenfeld," said Gray. "It's time for me to go home."

"Who? Who is this? You know this kid?" Drew kept steering his questions in Katrina's direction.

"She's from my party," Katrina answered primly. "Which, as it turned out, wasn't my party after all. I couldn't find my party."

"Party? Kat, we've been through this. I'll have a party for you when we're more settled. Next week, maybe."

Katrina clenched her fists in her lap. "You told me whenever I wanted it. You promised . . . and I thought you were tricking me when you left this afternoon! I thought I was supposed to come find you!"

"Find me? I said a thousand times I was going out with Tony for a while. I had some errands, I said. I *told* you." Drew's drawl was dropping into a low grumble.

Katrina did not say anything. So Gray recited her address and her phone number and her mother's car phone number and her mother's cell phone number and her father's work

number and her father's cell phone number. She was halfway
through Caitlin's address when Drew interrupted her.

"Okay, okay." He held up a hand for Gray to stop. "I'll take
you home. My girlfriend, Kat, she's a little, you know . . ." He
pulled his hand through his greasy hair. His feet were restless
on the floor. They carried him a little bit here and then there. He
turned to Katrina again. "You took the car and went out?
Where to?"

"Oh, around. The store, and then some roads with houses.
I thought I was supposed to find you."

Drew spun in a clumsy half circle and made a frustrated
growling noise. "You said you'd stay here and wait for those
guys to drop by. Did they come by while you were out?"

"How do I know if they came by while I was out? I was out!
Why are you yelling at me? I hate it when you yell!" Although
it was Katrina's voice that blared. She cupped her hands over
her face and began to wag her head back and forth.

"And where'd you find her, this kid?"

"I stopped by the party and she came out with me. She
wants to leave, but I don't know if I can drive any more."

Gray edged herself forward on the couch. She allowed herself to suck both ends of her thumbs, which she had been long
trained against doing. She needed food. She needed to use the
bathroom. She could feel panic crawling like invisible bugs on
her skin, and she wished she knew her mother's yoga breathing tricks.

All her life, Gray had obeyed the rules of grown-ups. The rules were work hard, finish homework, be polite, volunteer, and play fair, and all the future rewards—happiness, safety, and a nice college—would be hers to enjoy.

Under these rules, Gray's entire life until her mother got sick had made sense. And even after the sickness, there were rules. New rules, some not as easy, but they existed just the same. They existed along with old rules, these new rules such as don't upset Mom and don't cry and be brave for Robby and keep it down and please no more crying and we all have to pull our weight around here, Gray! were harder to follow.

She did try, even though she wanted her old mom back. The livelier, more fun mom that she used to have. The mom who took Gray and Robby to SpaceRollers restaurant on Sunday nights, the mom who turned raking leaves in the backyard into a family game. That mom always wanted Gray and Robby to experience things. Taste this soup, Gray. More pepper, do you think? Listen, Gray. That's a jaybird. Look, look, Gray, up at the skywriter! Oh, Gray, can you smell that awful factory smoke? Peee-yew!

Before she got sick, she had been more radiant with life than any mom. Always she had led the way, waltzing ahead and doubling back, circling and coaxing Gray and Robby into the enchantment of what she saw and heard and knew.

Gray missed her old mom, but she respected the new rules.

Not one single rule in her life had prepared her for this night.

Gray looked from Drew to Katrina and back again. The two of them seemed to shine with a jittery energy. Gray could not see if these people had RIGHT or WRONG stamped across them. They were mixed-up and smeary. They blurred.

If a real grown-up were here, the grown-up would know what kind of danger might flood this house. Gray could not tell. She tried but she could not grasp it.

"I have to go to the bathroom," she said.

Drew pointed to the bathroom door. His eyes remained on Katrina.

"I can't believe you went out," he said. "I can't believe you took the car and went out. After what I told you. Did you run into anybody? Anyone you know?"

"No, nobody. I'm sorry I went out," Kat answered. "I didn't think you'd be mad." She did not sound very sorry. She sounded as if she were speaking to finish up the conversation.

Gray looked from Drew to Kat and back again. Searching for clues and rules.

Would they take her home? Would they hurt her?

She didn't know. She escaped to the bathroom and locked the door.

She stayed in the bathroom for a while, searching. There was nothing to find. In the medicine cabinet was a bottle of mouthwash, dental tape, a bottle of pills to stop burping. On the windowsill was an abandoned spiderweb in which was trapped a husk that might once have been a small fly. On the toilet tank was an air deodorizer in the shape of a sleeping unicorn. In the shower was a piece of soap worn thin as a tongue.

These people no they are not bad no because if these people were bad shouldn't there be more dangerous clues lying around?

She could lock the door and stay in this bathroom all night. She could sleep in the tub. Shut her eyes and wait for her parents to find her. Maybe they were already on her trail!

She climbed in the tub and hugged her arms around her knees. Closed her eyes and tried to transport herself to somewhere else.

Right at this moment, she bet Martha Van Riet was saying awful things about her. That's what Martha did whenever one of the group was not around. Last week, it had been Zoë who was absent, and Martha spent the whole day slamming her.

All those terrible things she said! Like, "I could put a leash on Zoë's eyebrows and walk them as pets, ha ha ha!" And, "Have you ever noticed how know-it-all Zoë talks like she's got a stick up her butt, ha ha ha!" And, "You know, once I heard a rumor that Zoë French-kissed a dog on a truth-or-dare last year at camp!"

Ha ha ha! Ha ha ha!

Everyone laughed and said no way and that's so gross, Mar, and everyone sort of came to Zoë's defense, but not really.

Now Martha was probably slamming her. Caitlin would be

over-ready to laugh about Gray, too, since Gray had wrecked her birthday party.

The bathroom was beginning to feel cramped and suffocating. From behind the door was silence. Had Drew and Katrina left the house? Left her behind? Was it safer that way, to be here in this house without them? Alone?

Gray emerged from the bathroom. She saw Katrina lying on the couch, the remote control in her hand. Drew was standing behind her, staring sulkily out the window and biting the edge of his thumb.

"I'm hungry," said Gray.

Katrina nodded. "Me, too."

"No, I mean, I'm really hungry."

"Me, too. I'd like some chickpeas and feta cheese."

"You don't understand. If I don't eat something, I might faint," said Gray.

Although she had never fainted in her life, not even when she stepped on a glass bottle on the beach and was taken to the hospital, where she got five stitches. That afternoon was scary. She'd thought she might faint plenty of times. When she saw flies land on her blood that spattered dark across the sand. When the doctor, meaning to be helpful, showed her the black stitching thread. When she caught sight of the metal butterfly clip that pinched the skin back into place.

But she had not fainted. Not once.

She was not about to faint now, either. But if Drew and Katrina refused to give her something to eat, then she might deduce some clues about them. That they were criminals or something.

"There's no food here," said Katrina.

Drew was making a slow lap of the room, peering out each frost-smudged window. "If they came by and didn't see the car, I guess they'll be back," he said.

"Do you have a cell phone?" Gray asked Drew politely. She tried to imagine what was happening at the Donnelley house. It was cake time, maybe. Or presents. She wished she had put on her watch this morning.

"Why, who do you want to talk to? You can't call anyone right now. I don't need to add you to my problems." Drew dismissed Gray with an impatient glare. "What are you saying, there's no food left, huh, Kat? There's gotta be something."

"Nope." Katrina shifted. "I looked already. Hand me that blanket?" She pointed to the blanket Gray had left on the floor by the front door.

Drew picked up the blanket and walked over to Katrina and dropped it on her in a heap. "What's that junk all over your face?"

Katrina touched her cheek and spoke in her baby-girl way. "The ladies made me up at the department store. They did it for free, for my party. They gave me a free lipstick, too. Mango Tango, it's called."

"Kat, for crying out loud! There is *no party!*"

"Well, I think that's a shame." Katrina pulled her arms over her head and yawned. "You know what? I'm going back to bed." She shook off the blanket, stood up from the couch, stretched, and touched her toes.

"I could go see if there's some food in the kitchen," Gray offered.

It was as if she had not spoken at all.

It was just like that mean game Martha and the others played against her.

Drew returned to looking out the window, and Katrina shuffled away to the bedroom.

Gray slipped into the kitchen and snapped on a light that popped and blew. Now the trickle from the living room was the kitchen's only illumination. She opened the rust-edged refrigerator and inside found a sandwich furry with mold, a sandwich bag filled with carrots and celery sticks, and a couple of cans of beer.

"Whatcha got?"

Gray jumped. Drew had crept up behind her.

"Nothing."

He reached past her and hefted a beer. "Kat wasn't joking," he said. He swiped the sandwich bag, too. "This'll do us."

Gray nodded. Together, they sat down at a table-and-chairs set that looked better suited to ornament a pool or patio area.

The chairs were padded with spongy cushions, and the plastic-topped table was thin and frail enough that Gray might have picked it up and moved it anywhere else.

"Check the cupboard." Drew cracked open the beer. "This is my, uh, buddy's place and they're out of town for the week. Which is why it's lean on supplies."

Gray thought Drew might be lying to her. Aside from the spiderweb and dead mouse in the trap, she had noticed a lot of dust around the house, too, in places where people who lived here would have wiped clean. Also, the rooms all had a mushroom smell. An odor of things that have sat too long in closed air.

She did not contradict, though. She did not want to make Drew angry. She stood on her toes to open the cupboard. She saw baking powder and chili powder, salt and pepper, vinegar, and a dented box of crackers. She pulled down the salt and vinegar and crackers. Maybe she could use the crackers to make a version of salt-and-vinegar potato chips? That might taste good. In another cupboard was a saucer that looked useful for dipping. She returned to sit at the table and she unscrewed the top to the vinegar.

"You want some crackers and dip?"

"Ymm," Drew said as he sipped his beer. He set the can on the table and studied her. "Gray Rosenfeld, right? Rosenfeld. That's Jewish. I got a couple of Jewish friends. But you don't look like any Rosenfeld I met."

"I was adopted," Gray answered promptly. She had been told and had told others that she was adopted ever since she could remember. "Jewish people come in all shapes and colors," she added. Someone had said this to her once. She pooled the vinegar into the saucer's center and floated a cracker like a small white raft on swamp water.

"Yeah, and you don't look like any Gray I know, either." Drew put a hand over one eye, then the other, studying Gray as if she were an eye chart. "Nah. I never met anyone named Gray. But if I did, she wouldn't look like you. Nope, no sirree."

"What do I look like, then?" she asked, although she was not sure if she was ready to know. Besides, she did not like Drew's tone.

"I dunno. Maybe like a half Chinese? Or Mongol? It's your eyelids, see. How they bend funny."

"They do not!" She could not resist touching her fingers to the outer corners of her eyelids, which felt the same as always.

"You're small, too. Like maybe you're stunted, huh? Where were you adopted from?" Drew leaned in on his elbows. "Some malnourished country?"

Gray used her pinkie to flip over the cracker. It was soaked with vinegar and its shape bloated. She could tell that it was not going to taste very good. "I don't know. Not from very far away. Not from another continent or anything. I'm American."

"You sure?" Drew took another sip. Gray wondered if he was trying to provoke her on purpose. "You were adopted in

America," he continued, pointing his finger at her. "That's all you know for certain. Right? But you could have come from anyplace else. Originally."

"My birth mother lives in America, in the Southwest. I'm allowed to contact her when I turn eighteen," Gray explained. "And, for your information, practically everyone in the United States comes from someplace else, *originally*."

"Everyone comes from someplace, sure. But *you* could come from *any*place." Drew sat back and winked. "Chew on that."

"I know who I am," said Gray. She was not upset, not really—Drew was being a bully, like how Topher sometimes acted to Caitlin and Ty—but she felt her eyes sting a little, as if to remind her that she could be sad if she wanted. "What about you? What's your last name?"

"Doe." Drew smiled as if this were a joke. "Brothers, sisters?"

"I've got a younger brother. He's seven."

"He's adopted?"

"No."

"Yep. That happens all the time."

"What? What happens?"

"You know, folks try to have a kid and they can't and so they adopt and then they're relaxed and that's when they end up having the kid they want. Their real kid."

"I'm their real kid."

"Okeydoke."

"I am!"

"Whatever you say. Whatever you say, whoever you are, Gray Rosenfeld." Drew smiled. His teeth looked mean. They were too square, each one identical to the next one over, like teeth soldiers at attention against her.

Gray decided she did not want to talk to Drew Doe anymore. He was sort of a jerk. Also, he was a stranger. She shouldn't be talking to him at all as a rule.

She lifted the dripping cracker and balanced it on the flat of her hand. Then she shook a little bit of salt on top. The cracker dissolved on her tongue. When she swallowed, it was as if it had never been there.

"How is your snack, by the way?" Drew asked. "Looks retarded." After a second, he said, "Oh, you're ignoring me now?" He sounded annoyed.

Maybe it wasn't a good idea to anger Drew.

"No. It tastes okay." She would be nice, but calm. Drew did not need to know that she was too-scared of him. "What's wrong with Kat?" she asked.

The question startled Drew more than she thought it would. "What did she tell you?"

"I've been around lots of sick people since my mom got cancer," said Gray honestly.

"Sorry to hear."

"You don't have to be sorry." Gray disliked when people said they were sorry and made pitying eyes at her. "She's getting well. She's in remission."

Drew opened his mouth to say something. Then he seemed to decide against it. He took a carrot stick and twirled it like a pen in his fingers.

"Kat's been my girlfriend so long that I can't remember when things were different with her, or even if they were. She's a nice girl, a normal girl, you know? I'm tired of everyone telling me what's wrong with her. Everyone's a critic. Let me tell you—there's a million things right with her! The situation is never black or white. I'm good for Kat. I take care of her."

"Has she been in the hospital? Is that why her hair's so short?"

"Naw, she's not sick that way. She tangles it when it's longer. Twists it in her fingers and before you know, she's got a knot in there the size of a rat. I bought her that wig for fun, see. To show it doesn't matter to me. 'Cause long or short, she's always my girl."

Drew eased back in his chair. He was speaking to Gray and yet he seemed to have forgotten she was there. "When I visited her last time, we put on the radio and danced. She loves music. That's when it hit me, how right we are, us. She's always better when she's with me." Drew pointed a finger on Gray. "I got what we need for a fresh start. Away from the critics." His hand winged the air. "From now on it's me and Kat and nobody standing in our path. We're taking off."

"Okay." Gray squared her shoulders. "As long as you drop me home before you go. I live less than half an hour from here.

But I could walk partways, if you're in a hurry. I really want to go home, see. I need to. Please."

Drew smiled wide, a wolf smile, and shook his head. "Little Gray Rosenfeld, you're the last thing I need to slow me down." He stood up, tipped back his head to finish the beer, and then shook free a carrot stick from the bag.

"Maybe you could drop me home now?" she asked. "People are wondering, I think."

"Don't worry your little head about it. You let me do the planning. I'm gonna check up on Kat," said Drew. "Meantime, sit tight. Those are orders. Do not wander off."

She would not wander off. Where was she supposed to go?

Drew was intimidating, though, the way he liked being the boss so much, showing off.

Saying those are orders holding rules over me for the fun of it just to be nasty to be a bully.

Martha

Topher seemed restless. He had finished his phone calls and he wanted to go up where the action was. Martha could tell. She was restless, too.

"Rugrats!" he said finally. "I'll be right back. You know the drill. The three magic words are . . . ?"

Nobody answered him. Everyone was absorbed in the end of the movie. Topher frowned and muttered, "Everybody stay put." Then he took the stairs, two at a time.

Martha waited a few minutes, then stood.

"Drink of water," she murmured with a yawn. "Does anyone want anything?"

Nobody answered. Were they playing a game on her? Martha's pulse quickened. Everyone was acting weird tonight. Probably it didn't mean anything. Probably it was because of Gray.

Martha crept quietly up the stairs, across the hall and into the pantry, her spy nook. Through a chink of opened door, she had a view of the kitchen. Still crowded. Some neighbors. Officer Bird Eyes and Officer Mustache. The Donnelleys. Mr. and Mrs. Rosenfeld were sitting at the table. Gray's little brother, Robby, was flopped like a sack of potatoes on Mr. Rosenfeld's lap.

"She might have needed some time to be by herself," Mrs. Rosenfeld was saying. "Gray does that. This past year has been a challenge for us, but Gray, poor thing, she's taken it very hard. I could understand if she wandered off. Gray isn't irresponsible. Emotional, but not irresponsible. But truly, Officer, I don't think forgetting her coat means—no, no, I don't think it means anything."

Mrs. Rosenfeld's sickness had stretched lines across her forehead and pressed folds into the sides of her mouth. Her eyes were sunken into fleshy skin flaps. If people had not known Mrs. Rosenfeld before she got sick, thought Martha, they might have thought she was a grouch.

Mrs. Rosenfeld did not look like Gray, but Gray had inherited other things from her, Martha decided. Gray possessed her mother's tame manners; the same way of sitting with her hands cupped over her knees, the same way of lifting the end of a sentence so that it sounded like a question. Anyone could see that Mouse and Mrs. Rosenfeld belonged to the same family.

"Listen," Officer Mustache answered. "We've got a search

on, but we can't do as much as we want until daybreak. Tomorrow's weather is forecast for clear, and by then we'll have an aerial watch, the best dogs. We've got precincts eleven through fifteen combining forces. If she's run off, we'll find her. . . ."

"For God's sakes, where were you, Patsy?" asked Mr. Donnelley, turning on Mrs. Donnelley as if she had invented this problem all on her own. "When she left. Where were *you?*"

"I was . . . I was upstairs." Mrs. Donnelley cleared her throat.

"Upstairs? For how long? Did it ever cross your mind to go *downstairs?* Any one of those girls might have—"

"Whoawhoa. No need to get into that." Now Officer Bird Eyes stood. She was walking straight toward Martha. "Coffee-pot is out here, right, ma'am? Mind if I help myself?"

The coffeepot was in the pantry.

Quickly, Martha ducked and fled on tiptoes into the living room. Hiding by the front window, concealed behind a curtain, she pressed her palms, nose, and forehead against the cold glass. She looked over the smooth lawn, at the pink balloons bobbing from the mailbox like baby-doll heads, at the strong, alarm-coded, motion-sensored stone columns at the base of the driveway.

Right there, that was where she had seen the lady. That was where her secret happened.

She could walk into the kitchen and tell them about the lady right now.

No, not now. It's my secret, she told herself. Another thing had started to bother her, though, ever since Zoë had brought up kidnappers. Maybe the secret was too big? Maybe she had held on to it too long? What if she got in trouble? That was no good. Martha did not want to be trapped shamefully in the Donnelleys' kitchen, making excuses to police and parents, while Leticia led the party without her.

She would wait until the other girls had gone to sleep. Then she would let the police in on her secret and deal with all those questions. Yes, that's what she would do.

Martha moved from behind the curtain and tipped her head back to gaze at her own reflection in the window. In the darkened glass, her freckles did not show. Her face appeared to float in mist, ghostly, like a drowned girl.

What if something bad already was happening to Gray?

"You!"

Martha turned. Topher was standing at the door, pointing at her. "Get yourself downstairs, runaway rugrat. Everybody stay put, remember? You gotta understand, kid, this isn't a game."

Zoë

"Where is she? No kidding, I mean. Where do you think Gray went?" asked Zoë as they hopped around Caitlin's bathroom and bedroom, taking turns brushing their teeth and changing into their pajamas. The question had begun to bother Zoë. She had been so sure she would find Gray. She had been so sure that Gray would be there in the night, waiting for Zoë to scoop her up like another prize.

Now it was too late. The movie was finished and it was bedtime. And with Serena gone, they were down to a Lucky Five.

"Hmm, I bet she went for a long walk and got lost," said Caitlin airily. "I really hope nothing, y'know, *happened* to her. But if it turns out she went for a walk, I guess we're going to be pretty mad at her on Monday at school."

"Maybe she got taken by some*thing*," said Zoë. She chewed on her pinkie, her last nail left. Her parents would be upset to see her nail nubs tomorrow. Tonight she had undone two full weeks of not biting them. "A friendly something. Like a space alien. Or a shape-shifter. A friendly shape-shifter, though."

"Or maybe she went outside and she met somebody interesting in the neighborhood, and she's watching a movie over at her—over at that person's house," said Martha. "Gray has body odor, anyhow. Did anyone ever notice that?"

Kristy started to giggle.

"Oh, that's a super-cool thing for you to say, Martha, if something terrible happened to her. If she's *dead* or something," said Leticia.

Kristy stopped giggling.

Zoë looked at Leticia, whose eyes sparked with outrage. But Leticia knew how nasty Martha could be, Zoë thought. Everyone did. Why did Leticia seem ready to pounce on Martha for every little thing tonight? The others could feel it, too. Zoë was sure. Leticia's thrusts against Martha had thrown an uncertain voltage into the air.

"She's not dead," said Martha. "Don't be an idiot."

"Listen. Caitlin's right. Gray went for a long walk is all," said Kristy smoothly.

"Everybody better quit talking about it or I won't be able to fall asleep," Caitlin added. "I'm too wide-awake as it is. I know! Let's listen to one of my new CDs. We'll put it on quiet so people don't hear."

"And I'll be the judge," said Martha. "I'll rate the best danc-ing."

Zoë liked that idea. It was time for a new game.

Caitlin tore open with her front teeth one of her vacuum-packed birthday CDs and dropped it into her sound system. Soon the music had everyone dancing. All around the bedroom and in and out of the bathroom. Crowding and pushing and twirling and laughing and shoving and bumping and toppling against one another, leaving footprints on the fluffy pink car-pet.

"Pretend you're at their concert!" cried Kristy. "Pretend you're at their concert and you're in the front row where they can see you!"

Like butterflies, they bounced and flapped their hands and watched themselves in Caitlin's large dressing-table mirror and her floor-length closet mirror and her bathroom mirror, pre-tending.

Zoë used her first-place breaststroke movements and kicked her legs. She was strong, she would dance with the most en-ergy even if she wasn't the best. Endurance was how she won against Shelton—holding her breath the longest or staying in the pool the longest, right up until the moment he said how stupid this was, how it was just an immature kid game, which was his way of giving up. Shelton was a sore loser. Zoë guessed she was, too, but she couldn't help it. Winning got all the at-tention.

Martha sat cross-legged on Caitlin's bed and watched and judged.

"What are you girls *doing?*" Mrs. Donnelley's voice was so low that she hardly sounded like herself.

Zoë froze, startled. She watched as Mrs. Donnelley dashed across the room and snapped off the music.

"Mom! Don't! Every time my party starts to get fun, it's ruined!" Caitlin wailed. "Gray wouldn't want my party spoiled just because she's not here to enjoy it!"

"No, no. No, no." Mrs. Donnelley shook her head. She went to Caitlin and hugged her. "Now is not the right time for fun, not while Gray is missing. Everyone must cooperate. Let's get you girls in your sleeping bags. Kristy and Zoë, your parents will come for you tonight, but I don't know what time exactly. Until then, I think that the best thing to do is to settle down."

Something in Mrs. Donnelley's eyes scared Zoë, and the truth hit her hard, the way it always did. Gray had disappeared outside of people's reach, outside of rescue. This was not a game to give up when everyone got tired of looking. Gray was gone, really gone, and she might be in real trouble.

Zoë counted back. Five hours was too long a time to be lost. "I guess I *am* tired," she said suddenly. It seemed like a helpful thing to say.

"That's right, Zoë, thank you, yes." Mrs. Donnelley looked grateful. She tucked Caitlin into her bed as the others followed Zoë's lead and zipped themselves up into their sleeping bags.

"Good night and sleep tight, girls," said Mrs. Donnelley, giving Caitlin's bed a final pat. She went to the door and put her hand on the light switch. "Of course I'm certain that Gray is perfectly safe and fine, but she is . . . *misplaced* right now, and she might be scared. Why don't each of you say a loving prayer for her? Asking her to find her way home. I know it would mean a lot to Mr. and Mrs. Rosenfeld and Robby."

She clicked off the light and left the room, closing the door behind her. After a few seconds, Caitlin slid out of her bed onto the floor.

"I've got my flashlight right here." She snapped it on. The others sat up. Their shadows pulled up like dark flames against the wall.

"Arrr-oooh!" howled Kristy softly. She used her hand to make a shadow-puppet wolf. "Hey, Martha. Who won the dancing?"

There was a moment of silence. "Leticia did," said Martha.

Zoë scowled. Unfair! Martha only said that to get on Leticia's good side. Which was strange, actually, considering how Leticia had been acting awful to her tonight.

Was Martha scared of Leticia or something?

"No, I didn't. *Kristy* won. For real," said Leticia as if it were obvious. "She's the best dancer of us by a million. I mean, Kristy's been taking ballet since she was, like, five years old!"

Kristy coughed. "Since I was three," she said.

"If I won, that would be called *cheating*," said Leticia. "Right, Martha?"

"Cheating, like how Kristy wanted to cheat so Caitlin would win Enchanted Castle?" countered Martha.

"What are you talking about, Martha?" asked Caitlin.

"Yeah, what are you talking about?" echoed Kristy.

"Nothing. Forget it," said Martha. Leticia shrugged.

Zoë stayed quiet, but her mind whirled.

Leticia against Martha. Martha against Leticia.

The Lucky Seven was breaking up.

If it's Leticia against Martha, thought Zoë in a sudden pull of panic, which side am I on?

"This is bad for Gray, I guess," said Kristy, turning to Caitlin and changing the subject, "if your mom wants us to pray for her."

Caitlin nodded. "Yeah, my mom's not really into praying except at Thanksgiving and stuff."

"Can a not-Jewish person say a prayer for a Jewish person?" asked Leticia.

"I think you can say a prayer for anyone as long as they're American," answered Kristy.

"And Gray isn't really Jewish, stupid," said Martha. "She was adopted."

"Don't say Leticia's stupid," Caitlin reprimanded. "Besides, everyone knows Jewish parents only adopt Jewish babies."

"Yeah, I'm not stupid, *Meow*," said Leticia.

"Leticia, why are you calling me *Meow*?" asked Martha, her voice casual but cold.

"Because you're the little kitten who lost her mittens!" Leticia answered gleefully. Kristy and Caitlin burst into shrill peals of quickly smothered laughter.

Zoë chewed her pinkie nail nub and glanced at Leticia. Why? Why was she doing this?

In daylight, Leticia was so dark that Zoë could always spot her first. In the cafeteria, in the gym wearing her white-and-gold Fielding Athletic uniform, tall Leticia's black skin seemed to make anybody who stood next to her appear that much paler.

By flashlight, though, Leticia's eyes jumped out of the darkness, the black pupil defined against the orchid-petal whites.

Leticia, the shape-shifter. Black-and-white eyes staring Martha down.

Would the group split down the middle? And if it did, how would everyone team up, and which half would be better?

Who was Luckier? Martha or Leticia?

Right now Zoë felt too tired, too perplexed. She would have to wait and see. She would rely on her special, extra-sensory perception, because it was important to get this answer right.

"Maybe we should do a séance," she suggested. "Maybe that's how we figure out what happened to Gray."

"A séance. What's that again?" asked Kristy.

"That's when you hold hands and try to raise the spirit of

the departed. But first we need to make a shrine using things that belong to that person," Zoë explained. "To provide a way for Gray to communicate."

"You can only do a séance if a person is dead," said Martha flatly. "Which Gray isn't."

"No, but if, like, if she's in trouble, or got abducted even, then we could be the first to know," said Zoë.

"Abducted," Martha scoffed.

"Is a séance like playing Ouija board?" asked Caitlin.

"Except there's no board. You have to channel the person through your own powers. Like them." Martha grabbed the flashlight from Caitlin and pointed it on the wall at Caitlin's picture of the fairies and monsters. Zoë shivered. She never liked that picture. It did not fit with the other pretty things in Caitlin's room.

"No, that's not . . . they're only . . . come on, stop it!" Caitlin exclaimed. "We don't know for a fact that anything's happened to Gray. We shouldn't, like, hex her! I vote no séance!"

"Me, too!" said Kristy. "No séance, no way!"

"I vote yes to the séance," said Martha. She smirked at Zoë, as if she knew something that Zoë didn't.

"I'm tiebreaker," said Leticia. "And I vote no. A séance is creepy."

"Three against two. Sorry, Zoë. Sorry, *Meow!* I've had enough." Caitlin snapped off her flashlight and jumped up to go back to her bed. "Ouch! I just tripped on something." The flashlight snapped on again. "What is that?"

The other girls looked.

It was Gray's sleeping bag.

"If I were you, I'd take it as a sign," said Zoë. "Gray wants us to contact her. Please, let me try. Just for a minute, please? Please?"

Gray

Today was Friday the thirteenth, Gray remembered. Tomorrow would be Valentine's Day. What did that mean, to have a day of bad luck right before a day of hearts and candy?

She dipped a celery stick into the saucer of vinegar. She had stayed in the kitchen after Drew left. He had said don't go anywhere and so she didn't, even though she had been alone here for a long, long time. She felt the tears in her eyes but she did not spill them. She must keep hold of whatever bravery she had. That was always a good rule, although it seemed impossible, a joke, as if she'd slipped Robby's toy pirate knife into her pocket.

Even with the vinegar, the food tasted like nothing. Hardly any taste at all. It was like dipping food into the sea. She leaned back in her chair and chewed up the celery into its watery, stringy fibers and she tried to believe that everything was going to be fine. She swallowed the tasteless celery mash and took another stick.

Why is this night different from other nights? The question seeped into Gray's mind and made her ache in memory of last Passover.

Last Passover, when she had to give up her participation in the Seder.

Last Passover, when Robby had been allowed to ask the Four Questions at the table.

"Robby is seven. He's a big boy, Gray." Her father bent and hugged her. "I know it's hard to give up something you love," he said quietly. "But that's what gives your gesture meaning."

She had nodded her head in agreement, although her mouth set in a stubborn line. The Four Questions of the Haggadah was her favorite part of Passover. Already that night had been too different from other nights. Her mother had been at her most feeble, hardly able to stay awake, and the whole house looked and smelled funny. That was because earlier, Mrs. Caplan and her daughter, Jennifer, had come over to scour and scrub down the kitchen.

Gray had overheard them talking, complaining lightly.

"What a lot of work!" Mrs. Caplan harrumphed.

"Too much," agreed Jennifer. "We'll have to scrape it clean."

"Well, she can't be blamed. So sick."

They had attacked the kitchen, using bleach and ammonia they had brought, even going over the stove and windowsills with Q-Tips. All for the worst Passover ever. Gray's mother had not even been awake for most of the reading obligations. Her chin sank into her neck or pitched wildly from side to side like a boat at sea, her sleep trance a not-death that scared them.

Gray had watched her mother in silence. She had sat with the bitter taste of her own private questions filling her mouth.

Aren't you ever going to get better, Mom?

Why don't you just try harder, Mom?

Why did this mistake have to happen to you, Mom?

What are the rules if you die, Mom?

Robby had not messed up the Questions. His childish voice was slow and brave. When he finished, Gray squeezed his knee under the table and smiled at him. She did not feel toward Robby what Caitlin felt toward Ty. Gray loved her younger brother intensely. Loved him right from the moment she'd seen his squashed, angry newborn face and her father had said, "Gray, say hello to the newest member of our family!"

She set the example, and Robby loved her back. It was always with disbelief that Gray witnessed Caitlin and Ty's non-stop fighting. There was no place in Gray's house for bites or scratches or hair-pulling or tattle-telling or wet willies or Indian burns or elbow slaps or dead legs or, afterward, forced, fake apologizing with crossed fingers while Mrs. Donnelley said, "See? If you didn't fight, you wouldn't have to make up!"

Drew had tried to hurt her by saying that she was adopted. He tried to hurt her by saying that she was not really Gray Rosenfeld, not really Jewish, not really meant to be part of her own family.

*He tried to hurt me with his mean wolf smile but my mom and
dad told me about people like Drew Doe and I was Chosen not once
but twice.*

Gray knew who she was when she stood in her family.

With her friends, it was a different story.

"The popular group has two leaders and all the rest are followers," Annie Dearborne had proclaimed during that time
when she and Gray were friends. "Martha is the first leader,
Leticia is the second leader, and whoever they pick is who gets
to be cool."

"No," Gray disagreed. "It's not like that. Different people are
leaders at different times."

"Leaders are always leaders," said Annie matter-of-factly,
"and followers are always followers."

Gray had shaken her head. No no no.

Deep inside, though, Gray knew Martha was the leader of a
group Gray was hanging on to by the fraying thread of her
friendship with Caitlin. A friendship worn bare of what it used
to be, now that Kristy took up all of Caitlin's attention, now
that anything Gray and Caitlin had shared in common had
slipped away long ago. Gray suspected that Caitlin stayed nice
to her only because of their moms, or because of what had
happened to Gray's mom, but it wasn't enough. Pity would not
keep her in the Lucky Seven. She knew that.

Being friends with Annie Dearborne was almost as good as
being in the Seven. Annie was loyal. Annie was a girl who

whispered if your zipper was down instead of pointing and yelling it out like Martha. Annie was a girl who wouldn't blab to others if she caught you crying in the bathroom, the way Zoë had. Annie would not make faces if your sleeping bag looked wrong. Gray valued loyalty, too, but that quality never seemed very important to her other friends.

The moon broke through a cloud and shone into the kitchen. Gray stood up and moved to the sink. Sometimes the moon had a blue cast and other nights it was tinged orange, as if its core burned with lava. Tonight it was creamy yellow white, like a cheesecake that was the tiniest bit lopsided. Ms. Calvillo had told them in science class today that by Saturday night, the moon would be full.

"So remember to look up at the sky," Ms. Calvillo had said.

Gray thought she remembered having read a story about how a moon, if looked into directly, made people go crazy. She made herself look into the moon's single open eye. She might need to be a little bit crazy tonight. A good kind of crazy. A brave kind.

From another part of the house, voices rose. Drew and Katrina were arguing about something. Gray could not make sense of the words. Her heart began to beat quickly again. She did not feel brave.

She continued to chew her celery and stare into the moon, one wise yellowish eye in the darkness, until the voices grew too loud to ignore.

Gray found them both in the bedroom. Katrina sat in the inflatable chair. Drew was standing over her. In one hand, he held Katrina's coat bunched at the collar like a garbage bag. When he heard Gray at the door, he turned.

"You see what she did?" Drew asked. His face was angry, purpling. He shook the coat at Gray. "You see what she did? Ask her what she did! Ask her what she did!"

Gray caught Katrina's eye. Katrina did not appear to be frightened. She made a dazed half-grab for the coat. Drew stepped back and held it away from her.

"Katrina, what did you do?" Gray asked obediently.

"She took all the money. Our money!" Drew burst out before Kat could answer. "She took it and she used it to buy this ridiculous—coat!"

"It's a pretty coat," said Kat in her foggy, girly way. "It was for my party."

"Ask her how are we gonna get out of here with no money, no identification?"

Gray thought she did not need to ask that. "Katrina, can't you return the coat?" she asked instead. "And get the money back?"

"She can't prance back into that store!" Drew spat. "They'll be waiting for her!"

Waiting for her. Did that mean Katrina was missing? Did that mean people were searching for her? If so, it was good news, Gray thought. If people were searching for Katrina, then they would find Gray, too. Gray would be a bonus person.

"I said I was sorry. I wish you wouldn't shout." Katrina made another reach. Drew dropped the coat on the floor and kicked it across to her. "*You* told me you were going to have a party for me," Katrina pleaded. "*You* were the one who changed the rules."

"They're gonna come by looking for the money, and then what do we do? Then what do we do?"

Neither Drew nor Katrina was paying attention to Gray anymore. They were hardly paying attention to each other. There was no use talking to them. They were locked up in the enchanted spell of their own strange world.

She left them there. Light-footed, she walked down the hall and through the front door, into the icy night.

Whatever was going on between Drew and Kat, one thing was for certain. Gray was not in the middle of their problems. She was an extra. She was a tacked-on, last-minute problem.

The night filled the outline of her and colored her over. It wrapped and disguised everything, the shapes of the trees and the house and the distance. Gray stared at the cheesecake moon. It was late. Bedtime.

When she got back home, the first person she would call would be Annie Dearborne. Maybe she would invite Annie to her house for a sleepover. Annie would not care that Gray wrecked Caitlin's party. Annie would listen to Gray's story and ask, "Weren't you scared?" And Gray would answer, "Yes! Yes! I was terrified! I thought they were killers!"

How scared was she, honestly? On a scale of one to ten? Strength seemed to be draining out of her. Her legs felt jellied and boneless, not solid enough to keep her upright. Everything was too confusing. Noise was filling her from the inside.

On a scale of one to ten, maybe a seven.

If she screamed, if anything bad happened, nobody would hear her. Nobody would know.

Maybe an eight.

From inside the house, voices continued. Drew and Katrina had moved into the living room. ". . . have to pick up that little kid," Drew was saying.

Gray opened her mouth and made the scream happen. She screamed so loud and long that soon it stopped being a scream and bloomed and blossomed into something else that might carry on forever. And then it seemed to her as if the scream never had been inside her, after all, but was always outside. She made the noise go on and on, expanding outward, taking up all the air and space until it was as big as the night itself.

Leticia

"Gray, are you out there? Gray, speak to us!"

They had all joined hands in a chain around Gray's sleeping bag, which sat in the middle of them like an upright log. The flashlight was balanced on top, pooling a spotlight onto the ceiling. Leticia linked herself between Kristy and Caitlin so that she would not have to touch Martha's hands.

Martha glared hard at Leticia. No matter how fiercely Leticia stared back, she could not mirror the meanness in Martha's eyes. Double-mean now, since Leticia had crumpled up Martha's last friendship valentine—that dumb lie-cheat that Leticia had won the dance contest.

I can do this, Leticia told herself. *I can go up against Martha. People will side with me. Everyone resents Martha for one thing or another.*

"Gray, do you hear me?" intoned Zoë. "Gray! Speak through one of us if you can."

Zoë was too much, sometimes. Always pushing for everyone to believe in her. She was doing a good job, though. She was scary. Involuntarily, a shudder rippled across Leticia's shoulders, and she noticed that Caitlin's hand was clammy in her own.

"Good acting, Zoë," said Martha.

"Shh! Let her concentrate," said Caitlin.

"Oh, tell us!" Zoë implored. "Tell us where you are, Gray!"

"Tomorrow morning," said Martha in a regular speaking voice as if there were no séance happening, "when the police find Gray walking down some road, lost, whatever, and then she hears that we were doing these things, I bet she'll tell on us to our par—"

"Gray, I-I-I hear y-you!" Zoë's voice was stuttering and unnatural.

Kristy gasped.

"Do you really?" whispered Caitlin. "Honest?"

Zoë's head listed and lolled and drooped over her neck. "Shhh. She is t-t-telling me." Her mouth fell slack, listening. "She's telling me that she's l-locked in a very small space," Zoë whispered. "Like a c-cave."

"A coffin, maybe?" breathed Kristy.

Zoë's eyes blinked and rolled. "She says she is s-safe here? She wants us not to w-worry about her?"

"Oooh, where is it?" asked Martha sarcastically. "Get directions, if you know so much."

Leticia could sense that Caitlin and Kristy were rapt, listening. "She is saying do not be fr-frightened for her," Zoë continued. " 'Do not fear me! Have no f-fear!' is what she says. Oh!" Zoë dropped Caitlin's and Martha's hands to shade her eyes.

"What is it?" Caitlin leaned toward Zoë and cupped her shoulder. "Are you okay?"

"I'm okay. It's just—" Zoë exhaled raggedly. "Well, if you want to know, but you have to promise not to tell? Lots of people in my family have ESP. I grew up around it. It wasn't till now that I was sure, but I guess I have the Sight, too!" She pledged her hand to her heart and seemed to collapse against it.

"Oh, brother," said Martha. "I wonder if Fielding gives out a Best Psychic prize."

Leticia held back the laughter that burbled in her throat. Any other time, Leticia thought, either she or Martha would have caught the other's eye with a sly wink, and they would have burst out laughing over Zoë and her dramatics.

I'm going to miss being friends with Martha, she realized. In spite of everything. I'll miss laughing with her.

"My ESP is a secret, Martha," said Zoë stiffly. "So don't spread it around."

"Zoë, you should tell the police about this cave vision of yours," said Martha. "If you don't, I think someone else should. Unless, of course, you're making it all up."

Now Leticia caught Martha's eye in a different way. "Why

would Zoë make up having ESP, and why would you go blab about it, if it's a secret?" she asked lightly. "Why are you always going against people who are supposed to be your friends?"

Martha lifted her chin into another stare-off. "Actually, Luh-tee-sha," she answered, biting off each syllable of Leticia's name as if it were some bitter food, "I know for a *fact* that Zoë is faking."

Leticia rolled her eyes. "Really? And what makes you so smart?" But she could sense all eyes on Martha now.

"Because I've got some real information about what might have happened to Gray. Information that, unlike Zoë's, is one hundred percent true. If I tell it, though, you all have to promise not to inform anybody outside the group. Because it's confidential." Martha looked around the circle. "Promise?"

"Promise," said Caitlin and Kristy in unison.

"Promise," mumbled Zoë.

"Promise," said Leticia. Inside she fumed. All the attention had turned to Martha as if she were a magic lantern. Just the way she liked it.

"Okay. When I went to get the mail for Caitlin's mom this afternoon," Martha began, speaking slowly so that nobody missed a word, "I saw a lady at the end of the driveway. Her hair was long and tied back with a scarf, and she was wearing a dress and this ugly coat with feathers hanging off it. And she was standing near a dark green or blue car that I think was hers. She came up to me and she asked me who was having a party. She talked like a preschooler. She was weird."

"Oh my gosh." Kristy giggled nervously.

"You didn't give out my name, did you?" asked Caitlin. "You didn't say who lived here or anything, right?"

"Of course not," said Martha. "I didn't say anything to her. I'm not stupid."

Leticia shook her head. "If that's true you saw a stranger lurking around here," she said, "you should have told the police. Not us."

Martha breathed a patient sigh. "Obviously," she said, "I already told the police. In private, while you all were watching the movie. And they said don't tell the other girls because it's confidential. Pluswise, they thought you-all might get scared. See, I was trying to protect you." She turned to Zoë, cold-eyed and disdainful. "That's why I think it's funny that you *conveniently* decide to have ESP, but you *unfortunately* can't recall that lady." She yawned. "But whatever. Now you know. The real truth."

In the silence that followed, Leticia could feel Zoë's embarrassment.

"Yeah, Zoë. You were faking your ESP, weren't you?" Caitlin sniffed. "Faker."

"Yeah, faker," whispered Kristy. "Faker faker, credit taker."

"ESP is for real!" Zoë hissed. "It's not something to wish for. The Sight is a curse."

"A fake curse," said Martha.

"Enough, you guys." Leticia moved toward her sleeping bag. "If the police have a suspect, then they're probably close to finding Gray. By the time we wake up tomorrow morning, she'll be back with us. Anyhow, my cousin Bethany is psychic, and she can predict if it's a girl or boy on any pregnant lady. So *I* believe you, Zoë. Since you always figure out a lot of stuff before anyone else."

Leticia's eyes held Zoë's a moment.

"Thanks, Leticia," said Zoë.

Alone, staring at the ceiling, listening to the others settle down around her, frustration surged in Leticia's brain. Somehow, Martha had turned the séance to her own advantage. Somehow, she had pulled ahead of the rest of them and shown herself to be the leader again.

Was that story about the lady even true?

Martha's a quick thinker, thought Leticia. But so am I. And Martha shouldn't have been mean to Zoë, mocking her like that. Just because Gray isn't around to pick on tonight doesn't mean Martha should transfer her bullying to the next easiest target.

Leticia thought through her plan. Because it was a plan,

yes, it was. She saw that now. She was making a plan to split apart from Martha, and to split up the Lucky Seven, permanently.

She also realized that no matter how she sliced the group, she needed Zoë. Although Zoë was not a leader, she was always a winner. Zoë would always be Fielding's class president, Student Government president, swim team captain, and the girl most likely to win Fielding's end-of-year Gold Blazer. Best Everything of Everything, that was Zoë on record.

Off record, Zoë pushed too hard, she was too know-it-all. But if Leticia and Zoë were a team, Leticia could guide her. They would be the right combination of finesse and brains, and everyone else would follow them into a new and improved, cooler Lucky Seven. Only it would be another lucky number.

What she needed to do was to talk to Zoë. She would say the right things. She would win Zoë over.

I can do this, Leticia reassured herself. I had what it took to get in this group. That means I have what it takes to become the leader of it. I can turn the Lucky Seven into whatever I want it to be.

She yawned. She was sleepy. Stressed-out, Celeste would say. But if anything good already had happened tonight, it was that Leticia had proven to the others that Martha Van Riet was not as strong as everyone thought she was. That in fact, Martha could be teased, ganged up on, made fun of, and ignored just like everybody else.

She, Leticia, had been the one to show the others. She had torn down some of Martha's supposed strength. That had to count for something.

Didn't it?

Martha

Martha was in a fog, twitching inside thoughts that were almost like dreams. She knew she had to stay awake the longest so that she could sneak out and report her secret to the police for real. Dread constricted her stomach. She had held on to this stupid secret too long, and it had turned big and ugly and was squeezing her from the inside. Telling the others had been right for the moment, but had not shrunk it. In fact, now the secret was bigger. Now she had to let it go. Every minute she waited only made everything worse. She wished she had never seen that lady.

Why couldn't the secret just disappear?

She heard the clock chime and chime and chime. It must be midnight, she thought. She heard voices from the study, and the crackle of the police transistor radios, but Gray's disappearance and all of its chaos seemed far away.

If only she could put off telling until tomorrow. Uneasily, she drifted.

Light cut Martha's eyes and startled her. Had she dozed off? She shielded an arm.

"Ouch!" she hissed. "Turn that off!"

"Shh!"

Who was it? Martha propped up on her elbows, reached out, and knocked the hand that held the flashlight, jumping the light away.

"Whossat?" she whispered. She squinted. Leticia? Yes! A trickle of hope ran through her. Was this a friendly visit? She kept her voice neutral. "Teesh. What do you want?"

"I want to tell you what Celeste said."

"Celeste?" Martha's pulse jumped against reason. Was Leticia inviting her to come along on her visit to Celeste's college this spring? Martha knew a trip had been planned. "What about Celeste? What did she say?"

"It's a joke she told me." Leticia aimed the light, vicious and bright, into Martha's eyes again.

No, this was not a friendly visit.

"Well, it better be funny," said Martha, shifting herself into shadow. "Funny enough to wake me up for."

"Celeste said your freckles show up on the outside of you to let other people know how you're rotten inside. Like spots on bad fruit, like on apples and bananas."

Under the sleeping bag, Martha clamped her hands together, forcing herself not to touch her face. She could feel the sizzle of each freckle on her skin. She never should have told

Leticia how much she hated her freckles. She never should have told Leticia a lot of things.

"Like worms ate through you!" Leticia was laughing softly, hee hee.

She's trying to scare me, Martha thought, wide-awake now and fully alert. Like when we crank-called Ralph Dewey that time. "If this is really about the science test, Leticia, you need to get over it," she said. "If you'd been smart enough to get an A plus, too, I bet you wouldn't be so bent out of shape."

In the pause that followed, Martha sensed that Leticia was considering this. "Cheating on tests is only one of the ways you don't play fair," said Leticia.

"Speaking of unfair." Martha's hand snapped out like a jackknife. It caught and wrenched the flashlight out of Leticia's grip and turned it off. "I've got a joke for you. Maybe you won't think it's so funny, but here it is. I'm dropping you out of my group." She laughed, too, hee hee, parroting Leticia. "I see what you've been doing tonight. But I've gone to Fielding since kindergarten and I know every single girl better than you do. Everyone has been way better and longer friends with me than they have with you."

"Longer doesn't mean better."

"I could get anyone to go against you."

"You can't do anything. It's not *your* group."

Martha was silent. Was that true? She could hardly imagine the Lucky Seven without herself at its center.

"But you're right about one thing," said Leticia. "Which is that I don't want to be part of any group that you're in."

No no no, thought Martha, confused. Leticia was joking, right? She didn't really want out, did she? What kind of group would the Lucky Seven be without Leticia? Martha scrambled for the right words, the words to pull Leticia back on her side without actually having to admit that she was worried or scared or sorry for what she had done. Which she was, but the only thing worse than the pain of these feelings would be to acknowledge them.

"Teesh, we used to be friends." Martha despised herself for the yearning that curled up in her voice. "I wouldn't mind going back to being friends with you if you admitted how much of a jerk you've been tonight."

Please, Martha thought wildly in the silence that followed. Please stay friends with me. She'd never had a real best friend before Leticia, and she couldn't believe it was already over. It had been so fun! As if parts of them had disintegrated and recombined into a single, perfect person. It was a better best-friendship than Caitlin and Kristy's. It was a better best-friendship than anyone else's. And now it was over. Now Leticia had knifed herself apart from Martha, and she had turned into somebody completely different, a stranger Martha hardly knew.

"Good night," said Leticia. In the darkness, the quiet expanded between them, forcing their distance.

"You're such a loser," said Martha finally. "I was only joking.

I'm bored of you, anyway, if you want to know the honest truth."

"Good night," said Leticia again.

Martha listened to the rustling as Leticia crawled back to her sleeping bag.

Alone, she waited. Waited for Leticia to come back for the flashlight. Waited for Leticia to come back and tell her she was playing a game. She was so hot, burning up. Her breath sounded loud, as if she were alone in a tunnel. She smelled the scrubbed flower scent of her nightshirt and the soapy heat of her skin underneath. Everything seemed extra-real. She tried to pretend that she was made out of stone. Unmoving, unfeeling. But her eyes watered anyway, and when she closed them, she saw hot pink and yellow jagged lights.

Leticia was not coming back.

It felt bad now, but it wouldn't tomorrow, Martha promised herself. Tomorrow, she would start to hatch some plans against Leticia. Good plans that would show once and for all who was the real leader. Only she wished she could do something mean against Leticia right this minute. Some kind of revenge that would get the others on her side by morning.

She had to go to the police now, she had to tell, and yet the weight of the secret kept her pinned in place, helpless.

How had this night slipped so far out of her grasp?

Gray

Drew's hand smelled bad, like underneath a car, like gasoline. The hand had stopped her voice. Gray writhed and wriggled to get free.

"What are you doing?" With the force of his fingers, Drew squeezed and shook her head back and forth. "What's the big idea, screaming your head off like that?"

"Mrrmmmp!" Gray swatted and pried at Drew's fingers, sealed heavy as a guard bar in a carnival ride. Dizzying, sickening. Nothing budged. She jumped up and down.

"Look, kid, I'll take my hand away if you promise not to scream again!"

She nodded her head yes, yes, yes. Drew took off his hand and Gray did not scream. She was finished with screaming, for now.

"Okay," said Drew. He was too close, intimidating her with his chunky self. "You, Kat, me. We all gotta leave. My friends are coming back any minute, and they'll want money for this stuff they're delivering. But *poof!* The money magically turned into a coat, right?" His laugh was tight with displeasure. He seemed nervous. His feet shuffled back and forth like a boxer. "So, for my next trick, I will make myself disappear. And you're coming with us."

Gray quaked. "Can't I stay here? In the house?"

"Yeah, right. Last thing I want is some blabbermouth little girl putting the whole state force on Kat's tail."

"I won't talk. Promise, cross my heart." Gray crossed her heart. Her teeth were chattering from the cold. It would be safer to be inside the house than in the car. She'd hide in the tub, or under the couch maybe. If she got too hungry, she would eat the moldy sandwich and wait for the sun to come up. In the daytime, the answers would come clear.

"Sorry, Gray Rosenfeld. I can't take chances. Look," Drew continued, "it's not like I'll drive you the whole way. I'll drop you somewhere. But you can't be *here*. I can't risk it. Okay?"

Gray nodded.

"I'm going back inside to pull my stuff together. You jump in the car and wait. Kat'll be out in a minute."

"And you'll drop me off at a gas station or something?"

"Yeah yeah yeah."

She moved to the car slowly. Her arms wrapped around her shoulders. It was too cold to be outside with no coat. Was now when she should break for it? But break for where? She was too far away from everything.

Gray opened the car door and slid into the backseat. Of course Drew would drop her off somewhere safe. He had to.

Eventually, Katrina appeared. She was wearing her feather coat and her wig. She waved at Gray and settled into the front passenger seat.

"Katrina, do you remember where you picked me up?" Gray asked. "Do you think you could tell Drew to drop me off close to there?"

Katrina stared straight ahead as if under a hypnotist's trance. "What I like best about cars is the radio. I close my eyes and I listen to the music and imagine I'm in these exotic places, like Fiji."

Gray leaned back in the seat and fumbled with her seat belt. Katrina was so infuriating, like the Mad Hatter at the Wonderland tea party. Only, unlike Gray, Alice never turned into a crybaby. Alice treated the Mad Hatter as if he were a small, silly child. Katrina was like a silly child, too, but in real life, a grownup acting like a child was scary.

Gray wondered what the other girls were doing now. They were in their sleeping bags. Maybe playing truth or dare, or would you rather?

Would you rather eat five live caterpillars or would you rather ride the school bus naked? Would you rather live in a sewer or would you rather be blind in one eye? Would you rather have warts or pimples? Would you rather have one miss-ing finger or two missing toes?

The Lucky Seven would play this game until their stomachs were sore from laughing. But it was so funny to imagine even a single terrible thing actually happening to them. As if any-body would really go blind! Or get warts! Ridiculous!

Would you rather be kidnapped by strangers, or would you rather have your mother die from cancer?

But Gray wasn't really being kidnapped. Her mother wasn't dying, either. She was in remission. And in real life, there was no choice about what bad luck or what mistake you would rather have happen to you. It just happened, and then you would survive it or you would not.

"I think it's really unfair," said Gray, speaking up to Katrina in her most authentic adult voice, "that you picked me up from the Donnelleys' house and you didn't even have a plan to get me back."

"I think it's really unfair that you came along," said Katrina, Mad Hatterishly.

It was no use talking to her. Gray slumped back in her seat and waited.

After another ten minutes, or maybe longer, Drew emerged from the house. He was holding a fresh beer and a paper bag that he tossed in the backseat next to Gray. She peered into it. It was full of clothes.

"Ready for our road trip?" he asked.

Neither of them answered. Drew put the key in the ignition. The car leaped to life.

Gray hooked her thumbs beneath her fastened seat belt and looked out the window, trying to memorize the house, the road, and the trees. As soon as she was dropped off, or got away, or something, she would be able to give good descriptions to her parents and to Mrs. Donnelley.

Poor Mrs. Donnelley. She might be mad at Gray for a long time, for ruining her daughter's party. Maybe Gray could take Mrs. Donnelley one of her mother's "get well soon" gifts as an apology. Some soap or a scented candle or slippers. Mrs. Donnelley would probably appreciate a thoughtful present.

Katrina was asleep. Her seat was cranked back all the way and her seat belt was unfastened. Gray waited for Drew to tell Katrina to buckle up, but he didn't. He switched to his high beams. The lights shone onto a wall of woods.

Katrina yawned and turned her cheek. Reflected light caught the sparkle in her face. With her arm thrown in a long arc over her head, she looked like one of Caitlin's fairy paintings.

Maybe that's why I followed Katrina in the first place that's how bad I want something magical—something better to believe in?

Watching Katrina sleep, Gray remembered how she used to watch her mother as she slept in her hospital bed. The veins of her mother's eyelids were webbed dark in her pale skin, like the mold swirls in blue cheese. Gray would stare at her mother and wonder if she would ever wake up.

Drew belched, interrupting her thoughts. Gray leaned up toward the driver's side. "Drew? Drew? You're not supposed to drink and drive." Her voice was just above a whisper.

"Stuff it, Gray Rosenfeld. It's only a beer."

Gray sat back.

"A beer is hardly even alcohol," said Drew after another slurp.

Gray knew that was not true. She was too nervous to argue more.

Tears flooded her eyes again.

She should argue more. Here was the place where she should draw on any strength that might be buried inside her. Here was the place where the brave girl escaped from the car, got on the bike, the plane, the train, put out the fire, saved the school, the town, the dog, the land, yelled at the Bad Person, pointed to the Good Person, explained why the rules were wrong, and forced the tiny change that always made Gray wonder, *Could I do that? Is there enough bravery inside me to do this one small strong thing that makes a difference?*

And always Gray wanted to believe *Yes! Yes! Yes!*

Even though she doubted it.

Zoë

Before she fell asleep, Zoë said a prayer, since Mrs. Donnelley had told them to.

She prayed: Please, God, let me fall into a psychic sleep and in my dream I will be the one to see where Gray is and then I can rescue her.

Maybe it was God who was supposed to help her win. Zoë figured God was on her side for most things. Like today, He helped her spell *ancillary* right on the English test, and yesterday He helped her find her green notebook. God granted Zoë plenty of luck when she asked for it, although He helped Shelton more.

If her dream gave her some clues to find Gray, then Zoë would get more attention than Shelton, more attention than anyone at Fielding, and maybe even in the whole town.

Now she had pushed herself into a dream that was not quite

going her way. Swimming through murk, she had found Gray, who was stuck underwater in a dark cave, so it was lucky that Zoë could breathe underwater. The problem was that Gray was screaming and ruining Zoë's rescue.

"I've got you! I've got you!" Too late, Zoë realized the dream had turned nightmarish, because she didn't have Gray. No, in fact, it was just the opposite—Gray was trying to drag Zoë down into the cave.

Zoë's eyes snapped open. Her heart was beating fast. Sweat was sticking to the back of her T-shirt. What time was it? How long had she been sleeping? She listened to the room. Caitlin was snoring, but otherwise the room was quiet. Outside Caitlin's room, down the hall, the house was awake with muffled goings-on, but none of the noise suggested that Gray had returned.

"Hey," Leticia, on her side, whispered so quietly, Zoë could hardly hear her. "Are you okay?"

"I was having a nightmare," Zoë whispered back. She was still breathing hard. She flattened a hand to her heart.

"You were talking in your sleep. You seemed mad."

"I was?" Zoë yawned. Had Leticia been sleeping next to her before, or had she moved places?

"Yeah, and I wondered if it was because of the science test."

The science test? What was Leticia talking about? "Well, I think I got an A plus," said Zoë, trying to keep her voice non-chalant. It was unc to brag about grades.

"Well, guess what? Martha got an A plus, too," whispered Leticia.

"Nuh-uh. Martha never gets A's."

"Not on her own. When she asked to copy off me. I said no, so she went and sat behind you. To cheat off *you.* I thought you knew about it."

Zoë frowned. She hadn't known. It irritated her to think of Martha copying her test. Without cheat permission, even. But she did not want Leticia to think she cared more than she did. "It's no big deal, I guess. We're friends."

"Oh. I thought you two were in a fight about it. But I guess it must be about something else."

"No, no—we're not fighting, Martha and me. Why would you think that?"

"It's just . . ." Leticia turned on her side to face Zoë. Her breath smelled like bubble-gum toothpaste. "Just that Martha's been especially on your case tonight. Right from saying you didn't win Enchanted Castle when we all knew you did. Then telling you that you don't have ESP. She makes you out to be such a loser."

"You think? Do other people think that?"

"Oh, I don't know. . . . Listen, I'm sorry," said Leticia. "I guess I shouldn't have said anything."

"No," said Zoë. "I'm glad you did." Her mind wound back through the night. Now that she thought about it, Martha had been pretty mean. Worse than usual? And was Leticia only saying this because she and Martha were in a fight?

"You're sure she got an A plus?"

"Positive."

"And it was from cheating off me?"

"Positive."

"Huh." Zoë gnawed the edge of skin around what was left of her thumbnail. "Um, Teesh? Do you also think Martha made that stuff up, about the lady? Because I really do believe my ESP was right. About the caves."

"I don't know. I was thinking, though. Probably we should go to the police and tell them what Martha told us." Leticia's voice was the barest whisper. "Just to double-check. Don't you think?"

"Except that it might get Martha in trouble," said Zoë. "I mean, what if she really made it all up? As a prank or whatever."

"See, that's how we'd find out for sure," said Leticia. "If she was telling the truth or not. Because she couldn't lie to the police."

"It seems kind of a big deal, going to the police."

"So what? C'mon. It'd be like a dare."

Zoë rolled on her back. So what? "Maybe. In a few minutes," she said. "Let's make sure everyone is asleep."

"Hey, I wanted to ask you something." Leticia's whisper

lifted, lightened. "In a couple of weeks, my parents and I are going to visit Celeste at her college. They said I could bring one friend, anyone I wanted. But just one, you know." She paused. "Maybe you'd want to come?"

"Yeah, that'd be cool." In the dark, Zoë smiled and nodded. She knew, all right.

Martha

Martha had strained to hear what Leticia and Zoë were whispering about. Now it seemed that they had fallen asleep. Martha could predict what was going to happen, though, and it infuriated her. Tomorrow morning, there would be two pairs. Caitlin and Kristy, Leticia and Zoë.

Martha despised the image of herself at breakfast the next morning, being called *Meow*, being laughed at or frozen out, plus in trouble with the Rosenfelds and Donnelleys and the police.

She shouldn't have been so hard on Zoë.

She tried to put her secret out of her mind. Maybe she had just imagined it. She wished something else would happen. Something to distract everyone. Something to shake things up.

The idea opened her eyes. A hush of balanced breathing, like a soft ocean, washed in and out around her, its calm broken by the hovercraft of Caitlin snoring in her bed above.

All clear.

She slithered out of her sleeping bag, then groped in the dark for her overnight bag. Fumblingly, she retrieved her Kleenex-wrapped mothball and her other bag of candy and chocolate hearts. She tiptoed into the bathroom, shut and locked the door, and snapped on the light, which made her squint. After she stopped squinting, she looked at herself in the mirror and touched her face gently.

"My freckles are where I'm bulletproofed," Martha whispered to her face. It was a silly thing she used to tell kids back in kindergarten if any of them dared to make fun of her freckles. Only tonight she didn't feel bulletproofed. Tonight, she felt as if she had been shot with a thousand darts.

She dropped, cross-legged, on the bath mat. Carefully, she used the edge of her fingernail to push into the chocolate heart. She made a small dent that slowly cleaved into two perfect halves. She licked out liquid chocolate. Then she fit the mothball into the heart, neat as a toy surprise, and she closed it up.

She tiptoed out of the bathroom, out of Caitlin's room, closing the bedroom door quietly behind her. She tiptoed past the den that rumbled with voices of the grown-ups.

A fresh pot of coffee had been brewed in the pantry and the lights were on in the kitchen. She would have to be quick and careful.

Bumpo was in his basket bed. He raised his head to watch her. She paused.

Maybe this was not such a good idea after all.

But if she could make Bumpo sick, Martha reasoned, then she could rescue him. She would call for help from Topher. Best of all, they would blame Leticia, for feeding Bumpo chocolate earlier. And when she finally told about the lady, there would be potentially two people in trouble tonight instead of just herself.

A perfect plan. She dared herself to try. She was good at dares.

"Here, boy," Martha coaxed. She slid to her knees on the floor next to the dog basket. She scratched Bumpo's ears and under his collar, the way he liked it. "I've got a treat for you."

One single mothball would not really hurt him, Martha figured. Her parents were always cautioning about the dangers of this and that, but experience had taught her that nothing was ever as bad as they warned. The mothball would only make him sick. Sick enough to help her.

She held the chocolate heart to Bumpo's mouth. At first, she thought he wouldn't eat it. His pink tongue lolled and licked the chocolate heart absently.

"Come on, boy! Please!"

Bumpo sighed, licked the candy again, then took it between his teeth as if to please her. The mothball crunched in his teeth. He gulped it down and immediately started to cough. An awful hacking sound from deep in his throat.

Martha stood. "It's okay, boy," she told him.

She spun on her heel and ran downstairs to the family room.

"What are you doing down here?" asked Topher.

"I went down to get some juice, and I found Bumpo. I think he's sick."

Topher used the remote to snap off the television. He stood and followed Martha up the stairs.

"Dude! What happened?" He pointed to the puddle. "What did he barf up?"

Together, they inspected it. "I think that's chocolate," said Martha. "One of our friends was feeding him chocolate hearts earlier tonight. Leticia Watkins."

Bumpo stared at Topher and whined slightly. Then gave a giant, shuddering, teeth-baring yawn. Topher dropped on all fours to check Bumpo.

"It smells like something else," he said. He sat up on his heels and propped open Bumpo's eye to inspect, as if he were a veterinarian. "Poor ole guy. Poor ole Bumpo. Getting long in the tooth, as they say." Topher scratched and rubbed Bumpo, who whined and panted. "You want some water, boy?"

"And I want something to drink, too." She could stretch out her time with Topher a little longer. And maybe if she explained about the lady to him first, he would be so excited to break this news to the police that she would not get in as much trouble.

"Let me take care of the dog first." Topher filled the water bowl and set it in front of Bumpo, who began to slurp it down greedily.

"Poor Bumpo," she said. "Probably Leticia didn't know any better."

"There's lemonade and Cranapple and diet sodas. Or I'll microwave you some Ovaltine, if you want. That's what I'm gonna have," said Topher, moving to open a cupboard. "I should have known you'd be bopping around—Martha, right? Little Grasshopper! You've been jumping out of my sight all night. All the other kids are sleeping?"

"Yeah. The other kids." She leaned against the counter. When Topher said kids, did he think Martha was a kid, too? She wondered if Topher thought she was cute. She wondered if she could get him to believe she was, even if he didn't think so now.

"I'd like Ovaltine, too," she said, since it would take the longest to make.

"Coming up." Topher pulled down two mugs and the Ovaltine. He dropped three spoonfuls into each mug and filled them both with milk and placed them in the microwave. While he set the timer, Martha looked at Bumpo's throw-up. She could not tell if the mothball was in it, so maybe it was still in Bumpo. Would he still be sick tomorrow? He didn't look too bad. Definitely not bad enough to get Leticia in trouble.

She cleared her throat. "I've been trying to get a reading on Gray," she told Topher. "In my family, a lot of us have ESP."

"Is that right?"

Martha thought she saw Topher smirk. It made her feel

extra small and freckly. Quickly, she added, "Some people don't believe in it. I don't even know if I do, either, but I guess I'm getting worried about Gray."

Topher's face turned serious. "At school, we're studying all that stuff in the class I'm taking. Psychology. Pretty strange. I wish I didn't know as much as I do. About human nature and all."

"Wow. You must be really smart," said Martha.

"No, not . . . I mean, I get by." Topher rubbed his eyes. "My grades would be way better if I studied, put some effort in."

"Me, too," Martha agreed.

"Tell you a secret," Topher said. "You look like the type who can handle a secret, and it'll be news by tomorrow, anyway."

"What?"

"They think Gray got picked up. Abducted, you know?"

"Abducted." Martha took a breath. The shame of the secret flooded through her.

"Mmm-hmm." Topher nodded. "No signs of forced entry or struggle. But there's no sign of her, either. A kid who runs off gets sighted along the way. Cops have got nothing. So far, at least."

"Gosh," she said. "That's scary."

"She might have even let him in, is what they're thinking."

"Into the house?"

"Yep." Suddenly, Topher jogged a couple of steps to the

back door and checked the lock. He returned, grinning sheepishly. "Sorry. Paranoid. But it's wild to think, how you can buy a nice house in a nice neighborhood, and you can lock the doors, set the alarms, buy the big dog, everything, and still some kind of evil might find its way into your house. You're never safe enough, you know? It's never zero risk. Freaks me out."

Martha suddenly felt dizzy. She slid onto one of the counter stools. "Me, too."

The timer binged. Topher took the mugs out of the microwave and handed one to Martha. "Careful. Hot."

She took the mug. "Thanks."

"Sure." Topher yawned. "Not much sleep going on in this house tonight. There's a night patrol, but the real deal starts at the crack of dawn. Then they're gonna start a helicopter search."

"Helicopters!" Nobody ever paid this much attention to Mouse before.

"But know what? I have this hunch a phone call will come in, and it'll be somebody who saw something and then we'll sniff out a clue. There's always a clue. There's always one person who remembers something. I mean, if she was taken. Somebody sees something, right? A car, a creepy dude . . . well, not to scare you."

Martha raised her mug to hide her face. "I'm not scared." In her mind, she saw the lady again, her glittering eyes and yanked-back smile, wrapped in that feather coat.

She would tell the secret as soon as she was finished with her drink. Even though she was definitely getting in trouble for it. Helicopters were serious. She took another tiny sip of Ovaltine.

Bumpo shuddered and whined. His tail thumped the floor and his eyebrows knit as he looked at Martha and then Topher reproachfully.

Martha shook her head. "I told Leticia a million times not to give Bumpo chocolate."

Upstairs, something was going on. Was that Zoë's voice? And now footsteps were running up and down the hall, and people were speaking, moving with new energy. Mrs. Donnelley suddenly called down, loud and demanding. "Topher? Is Martha Van Riet downstairs? We need her upstairs. Now!"

"Yeah, yeah. She's down here. We'll be right up." Topher made a face. "Guess they discovered your escape hatch, prisoner. Back to the pen, huh?"

Martha shrugged her shoulders. She could not seem to find enough air to breathe. Her secret was out. Zoë had beaten her to it. Zoë, of course, who always had to win everything.

"Now!" Mrs. Donnelley's voice cried. "In the study!"

Martha was sick from the secret, anyway. Relieved, even,

that it no longer belonged to her. She set her mug on the counter.

"I'm ready," she said. "I'm finished."

"Yep." Topher knelt down to give Bumpo one last pat. "All right, doggy, okay, ole boy," he said. "You're gonna be okay. Jeez, Bumpo. I wonder what got into you?"

Gray

She pressed her head against the car window and watched the broken white lines on the road. They moved so fast, white black white black white black. Sometimes she saw the white and the black separated and sometimes she saw the blur, depending on how she watched.

She wondered where they were going.

What was out in the movable dark? Past her house and her friends' houses on the roads close by and past Knightworthy Avenue and past Fielding Academy.

"You can drop me off here," she said.

Now they were getting onto a ramp. Now they were on the highway.

"You can drop me off here," she said again.

Gray felt too-scared again. She was crying softly, hoping that something better would happen to her. Hoping that her parents would pull up out of nowhere or that the car would get a flat tire or that she would wake up from this terrible dream.

She wondered what happened to girls when they got kidnapped by kidnappers who hadn't planned on taking them.

Because wasn't she getting kidnapped, even if it was an accident?

Katrina was singing a soft song along with the radio. Drew was talking to himself under his breath. They were not real grown-ups, Gray thought. They had the bodies of grown-ups but inside they were fragile and see-through to their strange kid selves. None of their rules were right or fixed or understandable.

"Are you going to drop me off anywhere?" she asked again.

"Just calm down and let me think," Drew snapped.

She was not going to get the answer she needed. Maybe she was asking the wrong question. She wished she could think of something wise and calm that would lead the way to a wise, calm decision. All she was good at, though, was crying.

Crying was the best that she could do.

She started to cry. Loud. Her hands pounded on the window. Her breath and fingers marked the glass. "Let me out! Let me out!"

"Shut up! Shut up!" Drew barked. He glanced up at her through the rearview. His eyes drilled into her. "Stop being such a girl!"

Now she was really crying, and it was too hard to stop. Crying might be the best that she could do, and she could cry pretty well. She could cry great.

In the front seat, Katrina started to whimper, copycatting Gray, the way Robby had this morning.

"Shut up, both of you!" Drew yelled. The heel of his hand hit the steering wheel. "I can't concentrate!"

Katrina sniffled and hid her face.

"I can't help it!" Gray screamed. "I can't help it!"

In the next moment, the wheels screeched and the car skidded to the side, guttering into the shoulder of the road, nearly hitting the guardrail, and stopped. Drew slammed open the door.

"Get out!" he yelled.

"Here?" she choked.

"Right here. Here is where you're getting dropped."

"But there's nothing out here."

"It's the end of the road for you," said Drew.

With numb, icy fingers, Gray unhooked her seat belt buckle. Drew hunched over, shoving himself and the seat forward so that Gray could climb out of the car. "But where am I?" she gasped as she stood in the highway. Her breath was convulsing, tearing through her.

"Figure it out yourself, Gray Rosenfeld. I've had enough of dealing with you!" She had to jump out of the way to avoid Drew slamming the car door shut on her.

Outside, stunned, she blinked at her own reflection in the window glass.

There I am same old me.

"Gray!" Katrina yelled. She had unrolled her window and was leaning up and out of it. The wind spiked up the hair around her head like an angry cat. "Get back in the car, Gray! It's too dangerous! Please!" Saying Gray's name out loud seemed to have jolted Katrina from her usual dream state.

Now Katrina held out her hand. "We'll take you to a gas station. It's not safe to be out on the side of the road."

Not safe in the car, not safe on the road. It was a choice between bad ideas. Gray's feet chose for her. Stumbling, she backed off, then turned away from the car and ran headlong into the night.

Behind her, Katrina was yelling Gray's name, on and on, like a siren.

Gray did not turn around. She listened to the sound of her name but still she did not turn. Not even once. She ran until she knew she was far away enough that even if she had looked, she would not be able to see Drew and Katrina again.

Cars whizzed past her and she kept running. Nobody slowed down. Maybe nobody saw her. Her arms and legs chopped and swung, her lungs were fiery with pain, and she could not feel her face from cold. But she trusted herself, and from out of nowhere a wild joy burst through her. Health joy and life joy and escaping joy and running joy and rescuing herself joy.

"Little girl! Little girl! What are you doing?" The car had come out of nowhere to slow down next to her, its automatic window rolling down in one smooth swipe to reveal an older man, maybe around the same age as her dad, who was leaning halfway across the front passenger seat to talk to her. She glanced at him without breaking pace.

"Kid, are you crazy? Do you want to get yourself killed?"

He looks nice too but I don't know this man he might be Safe or not I don't know.

She looked away, waved him on. Too dangerous.

The man muttered something, and then sped ahead of her. She kept running. She could feel herself smile from deep inside, although her face was sore and hurt from crying, although she was freezing, and she wondered if this was her chip-scrap of hope, of bravery, the place inside her that knew maybe things were not going to turn out as bad as they had started.

What was Safety anyhow, but trust in the road she was running on? What was Safety anyhow, but trust in herself? She would run until she saw an exit for a gas station. She would not stop until it was okay to stop.

I know where I am even if I don't right this second I know where I am I'm right here.

On the other side of the guardrail, the woods lay thick and deep. If she had to, she could always jump over the rail, off the road, away from cars, if cars meant danger. She listened to her breath and the slap of her sneakers. She listened to the Safety that had come alive inside her, doing its best to figure things out.

Everything was going to turn out okay. She was making sure of it, she was watching out for herself, she was under her own protection. Even before the noise of the police siren grew deafening and the blunt blue light parted her from the darkness. Even before the squad car pulled close and stopped when she stopped and opened its door to fish her out of the night. Even before, Gray knew that the worst horror of the night was over, the worst of the night lived only in her memory now. And she had escaped it, she had survived it, she was on her way home.

Booty